DREAMS
OF BEING

Michael J. Seidlinger

maudlinhouse.net
twitter.com/maudlinhouse

ISBN-13: 978-0-9994723-5-4

Dreams of Being

CONTENTS

"I do the same thing over and over, improving bit by bit. There is always a yearning to achieve more. I'll continue to climb, trying to reach the top, but no one knows where the top is."

—Jiro Ono

BOROUGH HOPPING

*I*first met Jiro at the grand opening of a Manhattan restaurant. I don't remember the name of the place, because remembering names of streets, establishments, and even people had become the least of my concerns. I had been wandering the city most weekends, when work no longer cushioned me from the loneliness nestled in every thought and gesture. People all around me, within arm's reach, a wave, a single word spoken could be all I needed to be freed from it. A solution so plain as day, yet why did I only feel the need to actually connect with a person at night?

Nights were the most miserable, sleep thwarting my every attempt to pull myself under. I drank and I took pills, did what normally a person did to black out, deny threat of the outside world, but I would still be awake. If I drank, I'd end up feeling worse, migraine and the sort of nausea that left me on the floor, cradling the toilet, too afraid to walk away because I could throw up again, always crept up with little notice. If it were pills, I would end up in a partial state, somewhere between sedated and completely lucid. I'd find myself staring at a wall, off into space, gazing with eyes glazed over, as the very thing I feared made itself known.

I tried everything. When you're without any other solution, you fight the feeling by keeping on the move. You walk and walk and walk because somehow the thought that you might find something keeps the anxiety at bay. You see it chasing after, always the thought that you might see someone you know, someone might recognize you, the entire thing crashing down on you.

So I started walking the city. I walked until I sweat through my clothes and I continued to walk until I could feel the ache in my knees, my back, my feet. And then I'd walk some more.

The details don't matter. Everything takes on a malleable shape. The buildings all blur together, seldom anything that catches the eye. The crowded streets become impediments, and averting your gaze, making sure to never make eye contact, becomes easier with every consecutive block. People left me alone. Maybe I did a good job of looking like I needed to be somewhere. Maybe I just looked the part: lonesome, disheartened, a person out of options.

I usually started walking in the morning, though that day I couldn't be sure of the time. I began deep in Brooklyn, Atlantic Ave all the way up, over the Manhattan Bridge because there were less people on it, more room to be left alone, and the view of the city compromised by the train passing, shaking the entire bridge, made so much sense to me. You glimpse beauty at the same exact moment you grasp how everything is broken and it's okay that it all seems impossible. The bridge spits you out near the Bowery, with its garbage smell and the first time I am tempted to stop and look, Chinatown not too far from here. It reminds me of a different time, when I first moved to the city, when everything was fresh, new, and the writing came easy. Too bad it was never any good.

I walked a brisk pace, fast enough to trick myself into believing I had somewhere to be. I relied on my imagination to fool the world, and hopefully myself. Might as well use it for something. I hadn't written in months. Everything I put to the page I erased. Every single concept I pursued, like any connection to the outside world, soured

2

the moment I entrusted myself to its ideas, every attribute something I wanted not only to commit to memory but also know deep down, to the bottom of my heart.

The writing withdrew more with every passing day. I wrote pages about not being able to write, directed to nobody. I wrote notes into my phone, pretending it would be for the novel, the book, the script, the whatever-the-fuck I was "working on."

What's my "work-in-progress?" I would have settled for progress, any progress at all.

I hadn't a clue what (and where) the work had gone. If I didn't walk, I would wallow in my room, lights off, headphones on, a movie playing back muted, as I would drift and ride that slipstream of jagged thought and tender memory.

Sometimes I would catch myself crying, a silent swell, tears trickling down without notice. Sometimes I would catch myself talking to people on social media, words of encouragement and flattery all my own, given freely to the other person just so that they wouldn't go, wouldn't stop talking to me.

Most of the time I walked like I was a searching for a dream.

I walked like someone that had no purpose, looking only ahead, in hopes that something would undercut me and force me to know its every quality.

The line. Though I can't be sure why I stopped to check out the grand opening. An authentic Japanese culinary experience, the restaurant must have hired the right kind of publicist because people were wrapped around the block.

No matter what you did to try to pass, there were guards and other things in the way, a barricade here, what looked like someone with a camera filming something nearer to the front of the line. I didn't want any part of it. I loitered somewhere near the middle, not in the line itself, but amongst the onlookers standing on the opposite side of the barricade.

All around me I heard gossip, the murmurs, the hype. Apparently, it was a much-anticipated event, the place founded by a master sushi chief from Tokyo. The chef had carved out his own following back home and had set his sights worldwide. That meant New York City. That meant Leipzig. That meant the sound of a future chain, a corporate brand being built to maximize hysteria and revenue. That also meant it caught the interest of people like me, who had no interest in the culinary arts, much less the ability to cook.

I listened to applause from the front of the line, something happening, but like everything lately, I had no interest in being a part of the passion. I had lost mine somewhere along the way and didn't feel as though I deserved to feast on the passion of others.

We all wake up every day.

In those first conscious moments is the most important act of all: the choice to align and continue. The act alone might be impossible, because in bed, in between the sheets, you can hide only for so long, but out in the open, naked and in the shower, suited up and walking the street, you are judged. And I could feel their judging eyes on the back of my neck. Standing motionless in a dense crowd, I could sense I was nonsense to those around me.

Out of place—body and clothes inappropriate and smelling of sweat—or maybe I just wanted a reason to turn away and keep walking.

It is so much easier to walk away than to stick around and commit.

I asked the person next to me a question, not sure what I managed to come up with, but it was likely something easy, like "what's happening here?" The person gave me the shrewdest of glances, a once-over that started with staring at me and then through me and culminated with a brusque reply: "The best sushi you'll ever have. It'll melt right in your mouth."

Then she turned back to the crowd, the event in progress. I don't really know why, but the way she said it confused me.

What progress had I made? What was I really doing, in this moment, today, tomorrow, in life? I guess the interaction reminded me of my worthlessness. It triggered within me everything I had fought so hard, walked such long distances, to ignore and forget.

I didn't know what else to say so I said nothing. I stood in line, a silent and withdrawn observer, letting every negative feeling win me over, until soon I heard nothing but silence. The chaos and excitement surrounding me eclipsed like what happens as dusk approaches— the color spectrum darkening and fading just as the weather itself cools down, a cue to everyone capable to slow their breathing, exhale, and let go of the day.

The day abandons you, the night consumes you.

I had been consumed—all around me I wanted to trade spots with any one of the faces, I wanted to look forward into the future and know, in my heart, there was much to look forward to.

The crowd passed me over and soon I was at the end of the block, street corner staring nowhere in particular. I heard voices, or rather one, a man with a deep yet raspy tenor, the accent undeniable. But what careened over every chortle was the manner with which he spoke of, well, anything. The sincerity of each sentence caught me off guard. He spoke as though there was never a doubt what he said could be wrong, could be defeated and compromised by the opinions of others.

5

I don't know why I did what I did.

It wasn't like me to strike up a conversation with a stranger. He wasn't the founder of the restaurant, nor was he a man of passion. Rather, he was like me, caught in the orbit of others.

This is how I first met Jiro.

I would meet him again, plain as day, months later. And a year from now, after finishing this book, in these pages, I would meet Jiro, long after we had grown apart.

BEYOND THE SCENES

*I*told him I was a director, and then a writer, and finally a journalist. He asked me which one was the "one that paid the rent,"
and because none of it did, I opted for director. A director
sounded far more prestigious, and in celluloid there was still the idea
that money could exist in the scenes and worlds projected onto the
silver screen. I mean, it cost like $18 to go to a movie these days.
Writing an article or essay for a lot of sites paid $100, often even less.
Writing a book, well that's part of the problem. I don't know where to
begin. I have enough false starts to fill a dozen books but none that
could really give me a paragraph worth keeping.

I had to tell him something. Jiro wasn't the sort of person that would
just talk to anyone. I had imposed upon the conversation he was having with someone I would later discover was one of Jiro's colleagues.
I wouldn't remember his name until the fifth or sixth time I spoke to
him, but with Jiro, I remembered his name right from the beginning.

Jiro asked me, "What are you doing here?" It was as if he already
knew me. When I told him the truth, "I was passing through," he
didn't find my answer to be acceptable. I had never been so intensely
judged and yet, at the same time, compelled to continue being judged.

"What do you do?"

Not, "Who are you?" He never asked me for my name.

Rather it was—*what do you do?* What are you really worth?

And for that matter, are you worth my time?

So I told him I was a director.

A tilt of his chin, the clenching of his jaw, and the interrogation, "Are you trying to remember things or are you hoping to be remembered?"

Normally I would have gone with the more selfless, less egotistical reply, the one where I talk about how it's all about the craft, not at all about success. Nothing about my sacrifice had to do with popularity and fame. I directed and wrote and researched for the sake of achieving... I didn't know how to finish that sentence, so with a sigh I said, "I want to be remembered."

The colleague laughed. Jiro fixed a stare.

Nervous, I turned away and assessed the line. It had grown from wrapping around the block to reaching the next avenue.

As far as you could see, there were people all trying to be a part of something, to bring not only into their lives something more meaningful but also to take part in a moment determined meaningful by the many that choose to help define what it is that made that moment last.

You could say I was doing the same thing.

I found nothing in the would-be result—I had no appetite, never really did these days. I'd eat whenever I'd remember to eat, which usually meant getting something at a bodega at 4PM and then wondering why I feel so dizzy, my mind aching to conjure up even the simplest of thoughts. I couldn't pay for this meal and by the sound of it, Jiro wasn't going to either.

But it was all about the restaurant, how it was, in fact, more of a fusion rather than something authentic. The colleague mumbled something about authenticity being sheer impossibility, which shot Jiro right into a rant that drew me in, listening to every line.

Authenticity had more to do with reverence to the history of gastronomy than whether a chef mimicked the work of others. Authenticity was every bit a matter of maintaining the quality and deliciousness of a cuisine as it was a need to innovate wherever necessary.

"For this, Kazuya hasn't the means."

The colleague agreed while I heard myself say it before actually thinking it, "Then who really has the means? He obviously has some ability…" Jiro stared at me, icy, stone-faced.

Was he furious that some sad-looking person had the nerve to question him? Probably, but I kept going. "Like, he must have some mastery over Japanese cuisine if he has attracted so much attention. You don't usually get this sort of response if you're a hack."

I swore, at this moment, Jiro wanted nothing more than to strangle me.

"Well a hack could hide it well, but eventually it's karma."

The colleague laughed again. Jiro did not.

"What goes around comes around."

Instead, he asked, "What do you direct?"

He judged me once, twice, never stopped judging my every word.

In some sense, we are at the whim of another person's opinion. We cannot stop them from suppositions, drawing conclusions from the information at their disposal. I didn't really launch into this with the best of intentions. I started a conversation by interrupting one that was in progress, and now I was doubting the very thing that attracted me to the conversation in the first place.

I had doubted Jiro's own opinion.

"I…" the vacillation clear, I dragged from nowhere the first thing that came to mind, "I write and direct documentaries." Jiro offered nothing, the same expressionless glare.

"Primarily, anyway," I added.

"You document because you cannot design from a dream?"

I frowned, "Excuse me? What do you mean by that?"

"To produce something from thin air is far more difficult than conceiving of something that has already provided a narrative."

I might not know why so much of my life had fallen into disrepair, but I do know this feeling, the one I had upon having my would-be work doubted. It was a fire from deep within, registering first as anger and then a second later, as veritable defense. I defended myself, and spoke of writing and documentaries as a novel means for exploring a compelling story, "Because any story worth telling is one that has, at its very core, a deep sadness."

I told him I was a director of documentaries and that I was good at what I did. I told him I could find in any narrative the conflict necessary to make it compelling. And then I saw, forming across his face, the intrigue that wouldn't leave until much later, when he would discover I was an imposter. I told him I could spin *his* story into something compelling.

The colleague scoffed, "You don't need to be good to tell Jiro's story. Jiro's story is already good." Of course, Jiro said nothing, letting this pass, letting other people pass, the line beginning to move. A couple nudged us aside, one saying to the other, "The guy has been rated a top chef by Michelin, three stars." I had heard them as clear and plain as anything else that could be said, and I watched as Jiro listened to what they said. It was there that I saw it, the sincerity and passion with which he spoke of sushi. I saw it fuming to the point of absolute pain, the veins in his neck and forehead visible, his face burning a bright red as he shouted at the top of his lungs what he believed adamantly to be true. It made it possible to do what I offered next: "I'll tell your story."

Never mind the lie. You could say it was a lie because I hadn't filmed anything before.

But it's true I was, or should say I still am, (at least trying to be) a writer. The reason for my lie was not to deceive or for some grand deception where I would later say "I told you so." The reason I offered was because you could say I had nothing else going for me. My life, like my long walks, was going nowhere fast and this was something, not just anything, but something that could keep me distracted from the failure that haunted me. I was willing to wear the lie until it became my identity, and wear it out if it meant I could say I was making *progress* with something.

Right from the start, our friendship took on a curious luster, one of doubt and competition, and then finally one of deception and desire. We wanted so much from the work we feared, and in doing so, we used each other as a means of meeting in the middle. We would talk and walk the line of fabrication, demanding nothing of each other, yet questioning our narratives whenever we were vulnerable. I guess the one thing I had, not quite the upper hand, really more a secret, a fatal flaw, was the very lie that had allowed me to know Jiro in the first place. For every interaction shared, it occurred with the understanding that one day I will have produced the very thing he had failed to do: I would describe every detail of Jiro's mastery and I would do so in the form of a tell-all documentary announcing the existence of a hidden master in the art of sushi.

And in some sense, I would do so. But the camera, it would be all for show, never set to record, remaining like Jiro, in the dark.

Before we parted ways, Jiro asked for my contact info and told me he would reach out "if interested." A little over a week later, Jiro left a voicemail. You could say I had forgotten all about our interaction, but that would be another lie.

If you can't already tell, I'm a liar. It's one of the few things that comes natural to me. I'm a *damn good* liar. It might be the only thing I'm good at.

When you basically live a completely solitary life, seldom any contact with another human being, every occasion where you do trade words becomes a breakthrough, something you think about, analyze, and exhaust yourself trying to come up with a better outcome. You fixate on what went wrong rather than what went right, and this sort of obsession taxes you so dearly, you sleep for twelve hours that night.

But I actually fell sleep, so that's something, right?

The message he left was simple. "I would like to discuss your work in more detail. I am inviting you to dine at a truly authentic restaurant. The sushi is delicious. You can expect an email with details of where to meet." Sure enough, the email landed in my inbox minutes after receipt of the voicemail. The restaurant was in the West Village, and he wanted me to arrive at precisely 5:45PM. The promptness of my arrival was, according to the email, "essential to fully enjoy the Summer Omakase menu." He never asked if I was available, perhaps reading me like an open book, understanding I had plenty of time.

A second email arrived the following morning, three days before we were scheduled to meet.

Jiro listed out what would be served, along with a briefing on the do's and don'ts of eating sushi. "If you aren't familiar, it would be wise to be mindful of the proper etiquette. I would rather not be embarrassed."

Clearly, Jiro didn't think highly of me, and why would he?

The etiquette appeared simple enough.

How to pick up the sushi—if with your fingers, lift it up gently, a slight pinching motion. Do not attempt to lift it from both ends. It will come apart.

You could pick it up with chopsticks. That was my preferred method, mostly because my paranoia breeds all kinds of additional anxieties. You bet I could be a real hypochondriac if I didn't try to temper and control my fixation on germs, dirt, the thought that any surface, no matter how pristine, could have hidden to the naked eye bacteria or a germ that could nullify an entire life.

Crazy to think but that's what I can't stop doing: thinking, fixating, looming over the would-be disaster. And this dinner with Jiro could very well be a disaster. He could see right through me. I had to get it right. I had to win him over. Or not—my life would continue in its uneventful manner. But god, the thought of that scared the crap out of me.

Picking up seaweed wrapped sushi, otherwise known as a "battleship" roll or more simply a "roll," or maki, I remembered how you were supposed to lift it. Instead, use the same method as with the sashimi to keep its form and the contents of the roll from pouring out as you bring it to your mouth.

This part, I had no idea I had been doing it wrong all along. Apparently with regards to soy sauce, the sushi chef is supposed to brush the soy onto the sushi before serving. If that didn't happen, or you somehow want more (which shouldn't be the case), you're supposed to use some ginger, dabbing it in the soy, and paint it on like a makeshift brush. You're not supposed to flip the sushi over and dab it directly in the soy (whoops).

The same could be said about the rice. You aren't supposed to soak it in the soy.

You aren't supposed to turn the sushi over at all. According to Jiro's email, doing so makes it taste different, the texture of the sushi itself hits the tongue. I know I've done this a few times, and one of my exes ate her sushi this way every goddamn time, but you aren't supposed to peel the meat from the rice. You aren't supposed to pick apart the sushi. This is about as obvious as can be. The sushi is meant to be eaten at once, the entire piece placed in your mouth. In one mouthful, everything prepared is calculated and made to be a balance of flavors.

The ginger, which is called shoga (I learned a new word today), is also there to cleanse your palate between sushi courses. Eat only enough to wash away the flavor for the next piece.

Apparently, it's preferable also to drink tea rather than coffee or an alcoholic beverage, which displaces my intention to at least take the edge off with a drink or two.

I wondered if Jiro drank at all, and spent too much time (read: an hour) thinking about it.

You are supposed to eat the sushi immediately after it has been prepared, which changed the entire way I thought about how sushi is served. What about the sushi that sits out on conveyor belts, the sushi that's made and boxed at grocery stores? What about the sushi I ordered via Seamless to practice these rules (because no matter how simple they were, it was obvious I was going to make a big deal out of it)? If Jiro had anything to say about it, I was sure to hear of it.

It made sense to eat each piece in one bite, taking it in the moment it was prepared for complete freshness. The flavor changed the more it sat, worse if refrigerated for later. There was something about the way the rice tasted after I left the final pieces of tuna nigiri for later. I had to drown it in soy sauce to make it taste like anything, the flavor of the tuna itself muted and then erased by the saltiness of the soy. But that's how I liked to eat my sushi. My preference was to order a spicy tuna roll and then drench it in soy. I couldn't be seen with Jiro if I ate contrary to what was customary. He would talk down to me in a manner that established how much I had yet to prove.

But that was the main reason for my apprehension. I reread the email, memorizing what were essentially simple instructions. I cared so much about gaining Jiro's approval because I had never met someone so evident in their disposition and what they wanted out of every interaction.

It was refreshing to meet someone that valued his time so wisely. He would save it for those he deemed worth the share.

It could have played itself out differently. I could have been one of many just passing through, the kind of person you share a glance and a "good morning" and that was all, the shortest pit stops in this thing called life. But he called me. He left a voicemail. He wanted more from me, and sure enough, I would be there to pretend to be everything he might need.

Jiro could have asked me anything and I would have said yes. That's how desperate I was for some sort of human connection. I do wonder, especially now, if I had said I was busy that evening, would Jiro ask to reschedule? Would he have moved on, losing interest? It was predictable how mine would have passed. I would have walked the city again, and I would have inhabited the same spaces, the same routine, until I wore out even that. Perhaps I would have left the city in search not of reclaiming a loss, but of running away from the loss already dealt. I would have continued to be melodramatic, but in the least, who knows. Maybe I would have stopped writing and found self-worth in something I couldn't know until I discovered it. So much could have played itself out differently, but instead I buckled and gave into the intrigue surrounding this man. I wanted to know more about this man, and more so, I wanted this man to know me. If I had to live vicariously through the passions and productions of others, so be it.

You live this way so long, you become self-destructive, willing to risk every comfort you may have to feel something. And I'm not proud of it, but I ordered sushi every day leading up to our meeting, and every time I imagined myself as a connoisseur, a gastronomist, each piece brought to one's mouth done so with care, appreciation and respect for the magnitude of such a culinary experience. This wasn't supposed to be *just* food. Just as I would hope one day I could write something that a reader would devour with enthusiasm, this sushi through its flavors heartens the mind through giving sustenance to the body. I guess what I'm trying to say is I was trying to keep an open mind. I wanted my life to change. I wanted a life—and I had looked everywhere I thought I might find it. The sort of thing you read about

15

when a famous public figure is profiled by a magazine. Their passion is derived from an unknown. Their passion is almost always there right from the start. It is innate, from birth, or it finds you. *It finds you.* I guess I just hoped it would have found me.

NOW SEATING... TWO?

I arrived at the restaurant early, approximately 30 minutes before they opened and another 15 before the proposed time Jiro had given me. This was intentional—wanting so very much to wander around the vicinity of the area, as if by seeing the front of the building, feeling out the atmosphere of the West Village, and really because I hadn't been in this area for what felt like ages would relax my nerves. I preferred to be early rather than late.

The way I saw it: If I had to be there promptly at 5:45PM, I wasn't going to trust the MTA or any of their trains to be on time. Anything could happen and train delays exist as a prevailing worry to anyone living in the city.

Ever look forward to something so much you lose track of the details, the direct reason for looking forward in the first place? You might have thought I was on my way to prison by the look and feel of every gesture.

No, just going to eat with someone I just met.

We humans deal in judgment. Somehow, I haven't been the best with it, which only adds to my inability to deal. Talk about a vicious cycle.

Anyway, I walked around in circles four times, with each repetition adding one additional block until my radius was four blocks in length. Then, realizing I still had another 10 minutes to kill, I added another, walking five blocks until stopping short of the one where the restaurant resided. The trick here was to walk but not enough that I worked up a sweat. I had to look calm, collected, as though this was yet another occasion, another meeting of creative minds, in a busy and connected individual's weekly trek through industry.

I caught a look at myself in a window as I passed, my face already thinly shimmering with the sweat. Well shit, I thought, and a second time, aloud, enough that the person passing by glanced over. "Well shit." I had caught sight of Jiro walking up to the restaurant. I kept my distance, around the corner, visible to anyone that looked, but thankfully, still concealed by the steady foot traffic of this part of the Village.

I looked at my phone. I had two minutes.

Panic followed by actually, you know, walking up to the restaurant. I brushed aside any doubt and walked right in. If I waited any longer, I wouldn't have followed through. I would have given into the nerves and walked back to Brooklyn. It wouldn't have been the first time I ditched right as I arrived.

Jiro sat at the sushi bar. He regarded me without looking, "Have a seat."

Seated to his right, everything served would be first served to me. I didn't acknowledge the fact that perhaps Jiro had intended to put me on the spot. Looking back, I'm sure of it. At the time, I doubted myself, figuring I was overanalyzing everything, reading too much into every detail.

He wanted to get a sense of who I was. We sat there, sipping tea, as Nori began prepping the sushi. The name I procured by eavesdropping the conversation Jiro had with the chef, in Japanese, of which having no familiarity became a reminder I barely know the English language, much less having proficiency in multiple languages.

Have I mentioned how low my self-esteem was at this juncture of my life? Okay, good.

We didn't speak to each other. Instead, the meal began promptly at 5:45PM with the serving of an incredibly hot towel. I fumbled with it, the feeling of the heat against my skin was surprising, and not in a bad way. As though I were asleep until that very moment, the heat shattered through the barrier of my current fixations. The sushi had my full attention.

Jiro stared straight ahead, bringing the tea to his lips in calculated intervals.

I did my best to match his demeanor, but it was obvious to everyone I did not feel comfortable in this environment. Whenever I could, I caught a look at Jiro while trying to remain undetected. Maybe it was that I was too overwhelmed during the grand opening but the details, contours of forehead, the wrinkles chiseled into his face, the skin stretched tight across muscle and bone, all appeared new. Jiro looked as though he had experienced all that life had to offer, and yet he was still here, conditioned for another lifetime. The reverence of how he regarded something, anything, you might think it's the only object worthy of someone's attention. He remained undivided and sincere with every gesture, every action.

I watched as he picked up a piece of sushi, fingers barely touching either side of the piece, a mere second of inspection, followed by the entire piece being placed in his mouth. He chewed casually, without force, and though you couldn't see it on his face, there was something unmistakable. You could just *sense it*. Jiro projecting mood onto every moment.

As I ate my sushi, I matched Jiro's motions: taking the piece, two fingers, though I worried my hand shook too much, my motions too stifled, and at least in one instance, I tried to dab the ginger into soy to add a little extra and couldn't manage to retrieve the ginger from the soy. It floated there, drenched, hopefully unnoticed (yeah, right).

When the sea urchin roll was placed on my plate, I sat there staring at it. I had never had this before and it did not look appetizing at all.

Jiro chimed in, "It is customary to eat what is served to you."

It looked gross. I couldn't imagine liking the taste, but in my mouth it went. It took every bit of energy to stave from making a face, a pained expression as I swallowed the sea urchin. I was too busy worrying to enjoy the taste.

I wouldn't understand the subtlety of its flavors until months later, when I would encounter it again, by choice.

Nori served nineteen pieces of sushi. I was full by the eleventh piece, but continued to keep the pace, each piece of sushi made I had to eat first, as was seemingly customary. Jiro positioned himself as last, able to supervise and observe.

When one of the servers asked if I'd like an alcoholic beverage, I caught myself mid-nod, glancing at Jiro who looked right at me, as always expressionless, before saying, "Bring us a bottle of sake, warm." The server bowed and retreated into the kitchen.

What do you say—make a little conversation? There was nothing to be said.

Jiro folded his hands on the now cleared counter in front of us and spoke to Nori in Japanese. I listened to the sound of each word, imagining them talking about the meal, Jiro congratulating Nori and thanking him for being our chef. Turns out, I wasn't far off.

They shook hands. Jiro spoke, in English, "Many thanks for your hospitality."

With the sake poured warm and bracing, Jiro made a toast, "To the sacrifices we make to know anything."

Not quite tapping each other's glass, more so raising it into the air a moment before downing the warm liquid, with a sigh, Jiro whispered, "Nori has much to learn."

He wasn't asking for my critique.

Jiro refilled my glass, "We all have much to learn."

Downing the sake, Jiro said, "Do we ever learn enough to be reassured by our accomplishments?"

Now was the time to speak up. I cleared my throat and said, "If you think you've learned enough you're not really looking hard enough."

Jiro nodded just once, "Yes."

We sat in silence, watching an apprentice clean up after the meal, sipping sake, but only refilling when Jiro decided to pour more. We sat like this for a while, drinking another whole bottle of sake before Jiro spoke again, "Why would you like to document me?"

Instead of answering, I asked Jiro perhaps the most important question of all, "How do you know all that you claim to know?"

I surprised both him and me, by the boldness of the inquiry, the image of Jiro expressionless, patiently in wait, deciding whether to reply, followed by the words, delivered first in Japanese, and then in English, for me to understand.

"There is more to a life than the days it takes to live it."

More sake and then another question:

"Why would you like to document me?"

I took a sip. I was already feeling the liquor. "Because I want to know what you mean by what you just said." To which Jiro added, "How do you tell my story?"

"From where you feel comfortable and then we work our way into the riskier parts."

This is where it all started. Granted I had no idea how I'd accomplish what I promised; worse, I had no idea how long I could keep the lie going before it all became fact. For now though, I was drunk and getting drunk with someone that shouldn't have anything to do with me. Between drinking we talked about the basics of documenting a story. I bullshitted through it like I did most things, explaining the structure of a typical narrative, which I learned from the years of obsessing over screenplays and various novels. Jiro listened intently, and he even shook my hand. He looked me in the eye and thanked me.

"You don't need to thank me," I chuckled, nervously.

Jiro shook his head, "I must. So many stories go lost and forgotten. Now mine may have more than an audience of one."

Yeah, you could say I was devastated. I would let this guy down. And still, I would lead him on. I wouldn't even look back, no matter how much I worried about the inevitable.

What does that say about me?

Jiro made all the rules and defined our days together. Discussion would be largely one-sided, with Jiro speaking and me listening, pretending to write down notes. Occasionally I would interject with a question, mostly follow-up questions to the ones Jiro had already posed, the camera recording every word, every gesture we never gave.

I took the footage and dumped it onto my laptop and began learning how to edit. Most of the time I set it to grayscale and pretended I knew what I was doing. Black and white: oh, how dramatic.

The audio, it turned out, could be cut with relative ease. From there I'd run it through a transcription service, paying money I didn't have (hey credit cards) to get what I should have written down from the beginning. I would go through it, editing it for clarity, rereading it in search for the meaning that eluded me.

I would take a sentence like the following—

What defines the desire that directs your days?

And I would write comments, as if Jiro had asked. I wrote replies like I was his equal, the one equally being interviewed, the one sharing the spotlight in this doomed documentary.

I have no idea what I'm doing.

And then—

I guess what defines me is what defeats me.

I just want to know that what I care about is really what I care about.

Lately, I can't be sure. It seems like the space I thought I could improve has turned desire against me and made me to be a poor fit.

That's how most of it would go. I always kept an original, unmarred by my indulgences. Most nights I would send and receive a transcription and read through Jiro's outbursts in between getting lost on the internet, mostly Wikipedia, looking up random facts, firstly about sushi, but almost immediately about, well, anything.

Just a second ago, as I wrote the previous paragraph, I wasted fifteen minutes reading about the Super Nintendo Entertainment System, or the Super Famicom. I read into the reasons for Nintendo changing the name and the design of the console for the American audience when the original design was far sleeker and more attractive. More colorful too, with the controller buttons being more in the color spectrum and the American version being flat purple.

This was how much of the work, the would-be production, never actually happened. It was just me, wasting the hours, doing what I could to feel less alone.

That afternoon we spoke, first time "on the record," I didn't own a camera and so my official excuse was I borrowed one from work. Like most things, I lied about what I stole (the camera, from my roommate). I'm sure he wouldn't notice; he's seldom home on weekends, and Jiro preferred to conduct these discussions on weekends. For a long time, my roommate wouldn't mention it.

He noticed though.

People always notice.

People don't always mention all that they notice and see.

Jiro chose a ramen place, busy and with a line, up near Hell's Kitchen. The place was called Totto Ramen and what I remember most was how we walked right in and they made space for us.

But yeah, the ramen was incredible and probably some of the—

Just now, I got distracted by Twitter—in particular, a poet with a compelling pseudonym, ending with "Dopeboy"—and followed the trail of tweets until I ended up on Tumblr, reading poems by an entirely different poet.

This is how I overcome, or rather prevent myself from overcoming, my anxiety when faced with the demands of connecting with another person.

The server at the ramen place recognized Jiro, and without greeting, escorted us to a spot facing the kitchen. The server brought us food, miso ramen, sake, without being asked what either of us would have preferred.

Jiro commented, "They serve one of the best miso ramen in the city."

Perhaps this is what I *should have* preferred. It was equally jarring and refreshing to have had my own choices made for me. This would become a trend, one that I would quickly tire of, and it became one of the leading character flaws matched to the mannerisms, or lack thereof, facing and preventing Jiro from a meaningful connection.

We sat drinking sake and then slurped the ramen up in silence, my first meal of the day, and neither of us said a word. He slid a photo to me, one of himself. He must have been twenty when it was taken. "If there is any desire to the work you've done, there must be evidence in your youth."

I listened intently, never taking my eyes off the photo. The camera in my bag, the notepad with pen in my pocket, stowed away: I wouldn't take them out until much later.

"I would like to tell you a story. I would like to tell you my story. As I haven't the means to tell it myself, I will turn to you. My hope is that your voice matches mine. I bury the details like our chef," gesturing to the kitchen in the back, "buries the secret recipe in this miso broth."

"The story shall meander and you will need to find me somewhere within the meandering, for I will not be able to say with certainty the details that have led to the life I now lead."

Jiro shut his eyes, exhaled deeply, and then drank.

The bottle empty, I looked around for the server, yet the server was already there, another warm bottle. Guzzling it and refilling the glass immediately, Jiro continued, "I left my true voice, the real tale, in another country. This country has afforded me the ability to be a ghost. I would like you to tell a ghost story, give life to the dead. Can you do this?"

It wasn't a question.

Too late to turn back.

Jiro, evidently drunk, "Every Saturday and Sunday, as we are currently, we will discuss a specific topic. I will decide the topic. You decide where to place the details. I would prefer that you not look in my direction as I speak. When the camera is off, certainly, but you must not look at me as we discuss. Our discussion is not for you to take part. That is the camera's job. You will record. You will listen. If I need another voice, I will ask you to speak."

I didn't know what to do so I practiced what I had just been told—looking straight ahead, listening intently, voice silenced and erased, which was fine, I was already used to that, as Jiro slapped me across the face. I imagined it sounded three times as loud, the crowded restaurant turning and looking all in union, in shock. My first reaction wasn't that I had been smacked, or the sting of the slap registering across my cheek, but rather that others would look and judge. Reality was no one looked. No one cared: a life story.

It was as though Jiro had done this before.

"I am asking you to never make an impression about me unless I tell you to do so!"

Tears welling up in my eyes, I did all that I could do: I complied. Jiro was drunk. That was the excuse I gave myself; it was the excuse I would embody. It was an excuse that went down well, like the sake we would continue to drink, long after neither of us could afford it. I asked the server when I returned to Totto Ramen on my own why we didn't have to pay. He had only the one reply, "Jiro never pays. We have learned to accept it." The establishment, like many others, I would soon learn, felt sorry for Jiro.

"Tomorrow," Jiro said, before parting ways. As I walked, stumbled really, to Union Square, I received a text message. It was an address for another restaurant, somewhere in Alphabet City. I copied it, leaving the directions open in Google Maps, and impulsively returned to my Amazon app, opening it and deleting items from my wish list. It had become quite therapeutic to mindlessly deny myself these products. At some point, I wanted them but this was me saying, *not anymore.*

In everyone's Amazon wish lists, you see temporary desires. What Jiro asked of me was not the sort of desire you can buy, but rather the sort that you must build, each brick in the foundation as much a failure as an achievement. To set the foundation, you had to dig.

Jiro asked of me that I dig deeper, until I can no longer dig myself out without digging through to the other side. He asked of me to do this, and in doing so, he would be able to dig himself out too. The drunk version of me nodded along in agreement, unaware that we were already so close to rock bottom.

THE DREAMS PLAGIARIZED

*T*here used to be nothing scarier than the blank page and my inability to fill the page with words. I would pretend to write by copying whole scenes from the books I loved dearly, the books that saved me. I surely wouldn't be able to save them, so I plagiarized and at the same time duped myself into a false sense of being productive. I wouldn't return to the books. Instead, I would write what I remembered. I have a whole file folder of countless pieces like this. No way I'll ever get myself to delete them, yet I haven't a clue why I cling to what effectively are plagiarized dreams. Perhaps it's because I wrote them at a time when I was so positive I'd make a go of this writing thing,

Since then, well—look at what you see. I'm not that difficult to figure out.

The first actual day of discussion, I arrived as I should have. By that I mean I arrived over a half hour early, sweating it out walking in concentric circles around the neighborhood.

I made sure to arrive just after Jiro, as if it implied I wasn't as committed to this professional relationship. The restaurant was called Sake Bar Satsko. I think it's still business (much to Jiro's chagrin). He

27

did not like this restaurant and, much to my delight (and his), we spent the entire discussion recording Jiro dismantling the restaurant. Like I did with the books I loved, he plagiarized their entire menu, going one step further and dreaming up the "better artist" by providing admittedly mean criticism to each menu item.

I found it odd that we did not order sushi, didn't even speak the word. Instead we talked about shumai. "The flavor should be unified. Where is the flavor here? Should I desire something flat, I would have purchased frozen dumplings and deep fried them in my own wok, during my own valuable time."

I looked straight ahead, as was part of the ruleset given to me, and enjoyed most of the food Jiro found disgusting. Because my view included some of the kitchen, I enjoyed the increasing looks of disdain in both chef and sous chef (am I using these terms correctly? I still have no clue if I am truly capable of speaking of the culinary experience or if I can add gastronomy to my list of shit I am bad at) as Jiro vocally, and loudly, berated their hard work.

And we hadn't been drinking yet.

When they served the tempura, I devoured numerous pieces while Jiro complained about the thickness of the breading. I liked the dipping sauce they had with it, but Jiro pointed at how it had only one register, one layer of flavor. Nothing lingered of worth outside of the act of initial tasting. They offered a pork as consolation for the tempura not being to Jiro's satisfaction. He ate it with a fork because, "The bun itself should not leave a residue upon one's fingers. To combat this inadequacy, I am forced to sacrilege—eating the bun with a utensil."

I thought it was really good. The tempura too.

It was very nice of them to provide us with a free appetizer, and later, a free entrée and bottle of sake. Though, mid meal, a thought occurred—might it be that Jiro was putting on a performance? I mean, he was being "recorded." The sake at the end of the meal nullified any doubt.

In such industries, the customer is always right, and the establishment must appease for fear of a bad review. The food industry might just be one of the last arts truly capable of being destroyed by a lone bad review. The publishing and media industry, hell, even film and the art world, can get by due to creditability from those that do review, and provide criticism. With a restaurant, you could be destroyed by one Yelp review from a nobody.

A wonder, one that registers after the fact: Had they viewed Jiro as a nobody?

Me, sure, I am what I am, but the mystique that followed Jiro everywhere compelled an audience. At the very least, it begged others to listen.

Jiro ordered for us—tuna tartar and Korean BBQ beef—and he spat out the tartar after a single bite, claiming something I couldn't outright understand. There was indeed a lack of avocado, and moreover, the apparent lack of zest that should be melded into its innate flavors by way of the lime juice was replaced with a very, how should I say it—*wait, I'm not on the record.*

Jiro's comment was punctuated with disappointment, "This is tuna tartar, underwhelming tuna tartar. It tastes as though it had been prepared by a dull hand, conceived of hours ago. There is missing the element of freshness."

The BBQ at least, Jiro enjoyed enough to have little to say. Maybe he just needed to actually eat something. Ironically, by the time the BBQ arrived, I was full and didn't like the way it tasted. I had expected an entirely different sort of flavor. What, I couldn't be sure. Still can't.

The bottle of sake followed the meal and we followed it with two more, on my dime.

"This must be imperative to the story," Jiro mumbled between sips. He discussed how freshness is sublime, a necessity, hospitality as important to a meal as the meal itself.

He led me on, never cluing me into the actuality of the performance. He had warned me not to make assumptions, and to listen to his words like testimony, as though it were gospel, finding the narrative within those words, which in this case, yeah, I didn't know. Maybe he really did just want a free meal. He was getting it no matter what. When it came time for payment, Jiro excused himself, using the rest room, and it was implied that I would be the one to pay.

Placing the card on the tray, I did some mental math, wondering how much left I had on the card before it was maxed out. I would end up maxing it out during our seventh discussion, but at the time I thought I had far less to spend. Either way, I sucked at mental math, horrible at math in general, and Jiro would conveniently return after the bill had already been paid. It was all so practiced, the server with receipt in hand, Jiro's return timed to coincide with the signature and single-serving breath mints. Perhaps I wanted to forget that whenever it was Jiro that paid, it was really the restaurant comping our meal.

The reality of the entire thing was on me and my masquerade: This was a documentary after all.

Of course, the budget was my responsibility.

I kept a decoy in my back pocket—Jiro had never mentioned anything about royalties or the manner of how any profits would be divided. Sure, there would be no documentary, but already this deep in, to live the lie you need to believe in it.

I believed in the fiction I had crafted for ourselves.

It's something I do well, believing in what never existed in the first place. Hell, I've been known to fall in love with an apparition, a feeling unrequired, an idea that never was. This was merely an extension of it.

The way the evening played itself out—ending with the words, *I am drunk.*

There was already plan of the next discussion (despite Jiro never asking if we would be filming principle photography, footage to mix in with his rambling) and I had enjoyed, maybe a little too much, his deconstruction of the restaurant menu.

Yeah, you could say I had a good time.

The "production" continued in a predictable fashion: restaurant dining and drinking punctuated by Jiro's discussion about the cuisine. My attention was all that Jiro wanted and he controlled the discussion, exploring the error in every establishment, circling something to be critical about. Sometimes it was about the minimal menu options, a lack of diversity; other times it would be based entirely on predictability. Jiro wouldn't go into detail about how to make something better. Instead, he battered every bite with how it failed to make that increasingly unknown high-water mark.

It would go on like this for longer than either of us expected before the glow faded and doubt seeped into our minds, our every thought about the project.

For now, we were living in the fiction I created for us to forget.

One day I received a text from Jiro with directions to a restaurant, one I recognized, Benihana. I was taken aback, never expecting Jiro to choose someplace that had become franchised, which only increased the dread of it being another dismantling of the restaurant in question.

Another oddity: Jiro instructed that I arrive at 1:30PM when it had always been 5:45PM.

Initial reaction was worry followed by more worry, but I should have been used to it by now. Around 1PM I received a text from Jiro with the following "new" rules:

1—Listen to where you are told to sit.
2—Do not speak to anyone at the table.
3—Maintain composure and stare primarily at your plate throughout the meal.
4—lace the camera out of view, behind you [and he added in specifics, which happened to be a ledge, next to a painting and a condiment cart].

5—Do not order any alcohol.

6—Leave promptly after completing your meal.

7—Keep the conversation overheard at the table [a "what happens in Vegas" kind of situation is what I figured he met, and soon, oh god, I would be receipt to irrefutable proof].

I followed my instructions, the place so goddamn fake and predictable, the wood paneling, the obviously Japanese accoutrements, fake smiles from person seating me, and the fakeness with regards to pronunciation of menu items pointed out as special for the day.

"Enjoy your teppanyaki dining experience!"

"Thanks," doing my best to match each measure without being obviously uncomfortable.

I stood from my seat, and placed the camera where I had been instructed. I tried to ignore the couple already seated at my table. They watched and didn't look away when I caught them watching.

Because I had been told not to speak to anyone, I maintained my silence, but the real reason I didn't say anything was because I wouldn't have said anything even if I could. Too shy and frightened by the thought of being center of attention to, well, become the center of attention.

For the couple, they waited for the rest of the table to be filled, chatting to each other cheerily, clearly a new fling, all flattery and physical contact.

There was no sign of Jiro.

A party of four joined the table. I judged them on the spot. It was so easy to place them: Four college dudes in the city on vacation. "Tourist" could be read across their choice of fashion, heard in how loud and uncourteous they were, not at all concerned that their behavior might disturb anyone else at the table. "I'll have a Bud Light." Yup, figured them out.

When seated at a table, people speak of truths. Upon dining, people unwind the very nature of their personalities and minds.

32

At precisely 1:45PM, Jiro appeared, pushing with him a cart draped with ingredients. He wore the white and red uniform characteristic of the Benihana chef, complete with the red hat that made them all look so odd and nearly comedic in nature.

Jiro had trouble positioning the cart next to the grill and the entire table watched in disbelief as the cart nearly toppled over, saved only because one of the managers, who I will learn later, his name, Garrett, who I recognized in an instant as Jiro's colleague from the grand opening.

Garrett greeted the entire table and returned to supervising the operation of the restaurant.

A hush hung heavily over the table as Jiro started up the grill.

The tourists drank and made a ruckus about how one of them was a vegetarian. The couple kept to themselves, talking about whether to order from the sushi menu too.

I couldn't look away. I did not listen to Jiro's instructions. I'm sorry, I really am, but I couldn't look away, and from the tone of the rest of the table, neither could they. Jiro's every move appeared to be as though he were underwater. He took twice as long to cook the rice, and three times as long to cook the meat. He never addressed the table, never even looked in our direction. When he glanced at the list of, presumably, what was to be prepared, he did not confirm with each customer what they had ordered. His attention, or lack thereof, to the table and the performance was replaced with gentle care in the food's preparation. At every juncture, it was as though Jiro cooked in a vacuum. When the table noticed the withdrawnness of his performance—or lack thereof—they complained by asking direct questions, ones that Jiro ignored.

Continuing to cook the food, an unsteady, maybe nervous hand extending to place each helping to each plate, they accused him of being "fresh off the boat," unable to speak English, and then later, the couple's suggestion that he was deaf. I watched in disbelief, unsure if my stomach churned out of anger or embarrassment. For the briefest of moments, I wondered if this was all part of it, Jiro attempting to make a point. However, when the accusations and the laughter ceased and the table had drawn silent, I witnessed the truth.

They wanted to catch pieces of shrimp in their mouths.

They wanted that flaming onion mountain.

They wanted the egg toss, caught so predictably in the chef's hat. They wanted banter and pandering. They wanted to eat and forget all that existed outside this table. It was less about the flavor of the food and more about entertainment. If they had focused on what they were eating, instead of having fun at Jiro's expense, they would have understood the level of prowess Jiro demonstrated that afternoon.

The lone bit of mock-pity came from one of the tourists, "New York City is so expensive that the elderly can't even retire. They have to keep cooking motherfucking food."

At the peak of the table's banter, I caught Jiro half-glance in my direction.

His gaze never farther than the crest of where the table and grill met, I could see the subtle lift of his chin, the straight face that punctuated every waking moment, as though humiliation hurt just as much as any happy moment might. I watched as Jiro positioned for the camera so that there could be no doubt that it was indeed him.

After he finished preparing the meal, he returned the cart to the kitchen, without a bow. Likewise, there was no applause given and everyone finished their meals. They paid and left, going about their day, the embarrassing display already erased from memory. This hurt more than the slap, and it snapped me awake more than anything Jiro might have tried to do that evening to embarrass me. I sat there instead of leaving and, fuck it, I started drinking. I drank until one of the hostesses suggested that I do so at the bar. They were preparing for another performance and unless I wanted to pay another course, I would need to leave.

Why did Jiro choose to show me this, to see him this way? It was undeniably embarrassing. But maybe that's the point. *What is he trying to tell me?*

I am still asking this question.

I hadn't received a text from Jiro since that afternoon. The day I spoke with Garrett the silence had outlasted four days. I had no interest in dancing around the obvious. You just can't move on from such an event. The more I thought about it, the clearer it became—Jiro *wanted* me to feel sorry for him. And I did.

I guess I had expected more, as though I were the one to receive sympathy, Jiro more so the mentor, the one that got it all right, when really, this relegated him to the same category as me—that which had assuredly gotten it wrong. Jiro wouldn't contact me until I contacted him first, further proof of the manipulation.

What does a person do with that though?

And tell me this *isn't* emotional blackmail.

The question sent me back to Benihana, an evening when Garrett had mentioned Jiro wouldn't be working a shift, and I made sure to let Garrett know precisely the reason for my arrival.

"Everything Jiro does is calculated," said Garrett, thumbing through a bunch of receipts, the two of us in one of the back booths of the restaurant, by and large the conversation one-sided, with me uncharacteristically commanding the spotlight.

I guess I just needed to get this all off my chest.

I mentioned how I think it was all intentional, Jiro trying to manipulate me emotionally, as though he's expecting me to carry the entire friendship. Then I added, "Or maybe I'm just worried he expects something of me I'm not sure I can deliver." I stopped short of the source of my doubt, my insecurity. It was not yet time to admit I was a fraud. Oh god, just looking back at it now, this early on, already in too deep.

Nodding, without looking away from his calculations, Garrett agreed, "He's testing you."

With I sigh, I slammed my fist against the table, "Great."

"Jiro doesn't trust easily," Garrett leaned back, arms outstretched, massaging his neck. "It took me nearly a year to get him to apply here, and even then, he never did settle into a rhythm."

He shrugged, "Fuck, you saw it. It's maddening as much as it is so fucking sad. But he needs the income. At his age, he should be taking it easy but there's still a fire inside the guy. It's remarkable. It's why he can get away with what he does. And fuck, he can cook."

"How did the two of you meet?"

With some hesitation, Garrett considered his words, and then said, "Exactly how you both met: There was no Jiro and then there was."

He poured some tea, took a sip, "Why don't you just ask?"

I brought my hands up to my face, palms against each eyelid, "You already know, I just... I don't know."

"You feel trapped," he took another sip, "but that's what friendship is, and if he is going to trust you, he's going to demand your full attention. It's the least he can ask of someone, given all that's happened."

Raising my voice, I said, "Then tell me. Tell me what the hell happened to him."

Garrett looked pleased. He leaned forward, hands folded, and began, voice registering as little more than a whisper:

"Here at Benihana, we serve sushi too. I'm sure you know that."

I nodded.

"When Jiro first showed up for an interview, he wouldn't look in the direction of the sushi bar. He wouldn't acknowledge its existence. To this day, he won't speak to any of the sushi chefs." Garrett raised an eyebrow, "He doesn't talk to any of the chefs, but hey, that's once again all in that realm of trust and demanding a certain amount of it, you know?"

Garrett took a special pleasure in relaying Jiro's story, as though he considered himself lucky, one of the few close enough to the telling to make it trivia, not too far from gossip.

You could say I didn't believe it, but reading between the lines, I learned more about what made Jiro such an enigma, a broken being repaired via the distance and silence reserved for the pettiest practitioners of self-sacrifice.

"I had him cook from the menu. He didn't ask for instruction. All he wanted to know was what was the most popular menu item, and then proceeded to cook everything but that menu item. I was shocked. It took him two hours, but when it was all prepared, myself and the other managers had a taste. I knew right then and there that in Jiro there was a world unto its own."

In Japan, they refer to such disciples as shokunin. In America, we refer to such people as loners, losers, people living a solemn and simple life, obsessed with the very thing that can't love them back.

"He had redefined our teppanyaki, the very thing we've been known for, like he had figured it out on the spot. He couldn't look the customer in the eye, couldn't speak up when spoken to, couldn't even, you know, pour a glass without spilling, but he made food that seemed otherworldly."

You go through life with expectations. By all accounts, most people want things for themselves (I mean, duh). They want a partner, a social life, money for both, some sort of stability. They want that kind of stuff. The shokunin wants only to work. They desire only the purpose from mastering a craft. Their lives are matched to the purpose and ability to remain productive.

"It wasn't until after Jiro worked at the restaurant for a few months, and after one big fuckup where a customer got in his face, pushed him down, that sort of thing—I thought Jiro had broken a hip, Jesus it was bad—that he opened up to me. He stuck around after closing that night and told me as much as he could, but it was clear he couldn't fully explain it in words, which is probably why he turned to me, and now turned to you. He told me he was a disgrace. He told me he fled Japan because he was a disgrace."

Garrett paused for impact, eyes beaming bright, "And he said that his restaurant was doing well but the funder turned out to be yakuza."

Again, he paused, expecting a reaction from me. Receiving none, he continued, "The restaurant was a yakuza laundering operation and shit really fell apart when Jiro found out. Shit went down and then they decided Jiro owed them money, a substantial amount of money. They took everything from him and he fled the only way he could— to here, the US."

Finishing his tea, Garrett snickered, "Jiro was a dead man. And he never saw his wife or kids or whatever again. It's the kind of story you hear about in action flicks, but there isn't any action here, just straight up sadness, straight up heartache. It's why I'll do anything for the guy. It's why he should be fired but he still cooks. It's why I'll take a call from Jiro whenever, doesn't matter if it's 2AM or midday. I'll be there. Nobody else is."

Garrett rested a hand on my shoulder, "Maybe that's no longer true."

The story, I couldn't leave—I researched whatever I could, stumbling upon the term, shokunin, and from there my mind could think of nothing else. Jiro was fascinating because he fit so poorly into the constructs of logic and society. And beyond the fickle, surface level shit, he clearly understood the craft of choice, the eye of his obsession.

Did that really happen?

Or was Garrett bullshitting me?

I wandered around the city again, my gaze grafted to the sidewalk, bumping into people, listening to the banter, the lashing of angst, people bestowed on what was obviously chance, an accident. I looked for Jiro in the streets. The more I walked, the more certain I became that one of the people I bumped into would be him.

I walked the city until midnight, my legs burning, feet aching, and then I walked the bridge twice before calling an Uber. I looked for some semblance of myself in his story. I labored over our similarities, or lack thereof.

A person must consider what it means to risk it all and fail. Would you regret risking what might have been there to save you along the way, yet sacrificed in the face of opportunity? Art and science ask of the practitioner their life. To get it right, and to give it your all, you make that choice.

Success demanded sacrifice.

The story of trying and failing is something you don't want to tell. But you have no choice but to tell it, figuring it may be the only story that's truly yours.

TRADING TIDES

A couple days limped by in a daze. A trance punctuated with the ending credits of films I had put on and forgot to watch, snapped from my thoughts as names of the director and countless producers scrolled by. Had they sacrificed the way Jiro conceivably did? What does it take for a person when putting your full heart in the project of your dreams? How does a person fall in love with their work? Do they always carry this adoration for their craft?

Text Jiro. Early one Friday evening, I did just that, offering a simple hello, a direct way of getting back to where our discussions had been bookmarked while remaining noncommittal.

"Are you okay?"

Jiro typing, followed by the question, "You have been busy. Have you been writing?"

I lied, "Yup, nonstop."

"Show me."

My stomach sank, needed something, a diversion, anything.

Sensing my hesitation, Jiro added, "How is the filming coming along?"

Cover up by asking Jiro a question about the filming itself—"Yeah about that. That day, umm at Benihana... I am kind of at a loss as to what to do with the footage."

Jiro began typing, but I wanted to get everything out before he interrupted, "Currently what we have is a lot of footage of you critiquing other establishments, which could be good as part of the opening credits, which is what I'm thinking. We're going to need you to address the camera more, and get more of your story out by—well, telling it."

"Is the footage from work adequate?"

I texted back, "It's harrowing, and if you'll allow me to be completely honest—"

Jiro texted back a "thumbs up" emoji. Okay.

"This is the sort of scene in a documentary that anchors a larger point. I would use this footage to present the main conflict and point of the documentary."

I waited, wanting Jiro to tell me, rather than have me assume something I might regret saying later. But nothing about how Jiro conducted anything was conventional.

Just say it. This is where we anchor all that went wrong, the telling of his tragedy beginning with the present outcome, working a job that wouldn't be demeaning in theory, but had become exactly that for him, someone that closeted an entire life, a master of his craft relegated to being hateful and disdainful of other cuisine, the more successful the more he dismantled it, having to prove a point wherein it isn't that they are peddling bad food. Rather, he needed to prove to whoever would listen that he could do better.

A characteristic feature and flaw of Jiro's was the deciding factor that he could always do better than anyone else. To be this way, a person must have a gateway to a personal hell in constant threat of being reopened, sending them to a deep despair.

But we had begun talking again, and I had successfully thwarted his inquiries about my writing and the production itself, instead my question about desire, or rather why "it could be so palpable some days, while others my desire to create felt as heavy as concrete," launched what could be a good interlude for the documentary itself.

This was the first time I had seen Jiro converse with me in a manner that almost made us equals.

He said, "Once you decide the make of your desire, you let it dominate you. You have to fall in love with what will never love you back."

I said, "And for you it was sushi."

He said, "I fell in love with sushi. I had so many ideas. My ideas continue to follow me. I would dream of sushi in my sleep."

I said, "I knew I wanted to be a writer the moment I read a book cover to cover, surprised that an entire day had disappeared and it was like I had escaped reality."

He said, "When I created, I could have escaped all that had been a bother. I was at peace when making sushi."

I said, "I guess I wanted to create a world, a life, a love, a character, a friend, a situation I believed I would never find in my own. I don't believe I deserve the real thing."

He offered, "You deserve a purpose. Everyone deserves a purpose."

This is where I identify the first instance of Jiro and I speaking as colleagues, as human beings, instead of Jiro commanding, instead our conversation was just that, a conversation.

I countered, "What if the thing you choose doesn't choose you back?"

He answered, "It is yours to accept. You spend the rest of your life proving it to be true."

I said, "And that's where desire and passion come in."

"Both desire and passion glow and fade, moving in and out of a life in waves. Purpose is universal—you must maintain your selection."

Did Jiro just misquote himself? During one of our first "discussions" he proclaimed passion to be the essence of devotion to your craft.

I said, "Are you drinking? I am drinking."

"It is 7:17PM. At this hour, I have begun drinking for the evening."

"Oh, the things we do to forget."

He said, "We need to deceive our desires to rekindle them."

"Yeah, distraction becomes a desire all its own. If I had to think about all this stuff all the time, I would go insane. Oh wait..."

"Insanity is a word given to people like us by those that would rather designate work as a means of employment and less a life's calling."

You bet I acknowledged that he said "us" rather than the singular, "I / him."

"I am insane," I said.

"My insanity has brought me a desire all my own."

"I'm hungry."

He asked, "There are certain traits to the person achieving excellence. Do you know them?"

"I can't say I have but I bet one of them involves sacrifice, right?"

"I shall explain by way of my craft. There are attributes to an accomplished chef. They must take their work seriously. They may be awarded numerous accolades, but the work comes first."

"Yeah," I said, "popularity is a profound distraction. I mean I think it is, I wouldn't know. But it seems like artists get big and then the lose focus."

"The second attribute is improvement. The chef continues to improve their skills. Never is there a moment in their career where success breeds satisfaction in one's skillset. You must practice and improve for as long as you live."

"This I agree with. If you think you've done all that you can do, you're limiting yourself."

"Thirdly, the chef aspires for pristine workspace, all that they do, it must be clean, and to the highest level of proficiency and care in one's utensils."

I tried to change the subject, "Is this why you had us go to all these different restaurants?"

He ignored me, "The fourth one is, in fact, one of the first attributes I perceived in you. Impatience. The greatest of chefs focus on ideals, on the idea that is theirs, and aren't the best collaborators."

"I'm impatient?"

Again, he ignored me, "It must be one way not the other."

"Is this why you had us go to all these different restaurants?"

He said, "The final attribute is that the chef must be passionate. Passion must exist in what has been done as much as it must exist in what one must still do."

Testament to my impatience, I asked again, "Is this why you had us go to all these different restaurants?"

He said nothing.

"Jiro?"

"These attributes coexist and yet, if one exists, they will be tested. It will feel at times like existence isn't necessary."

"And that's why we went to all those restaurants."

"To become a dream you must live through the nightmare."

"This conversation," I said, "if it were a scene, should end with that statement."

"Proclaimed the writer," he said.

Not a single word more, the texts stopped. In a room all by myself, I laughed. Off the record, I was laughing. Jiro had made me laugh. I haven't mentioned it since.

On this very page, it will be the only time I ever do.

Jiro wasn't the type of person to let things go. On the morning of what was to be our next discussion, next would-be filming, instead of instructions I received accusations.

"I have searched the internet using your name. I have found nothing to corroborate your publication and film history."

I sat there in disbelief, unsure of how to move forward, having been put on the spot.

"If I were to trust the internet, you do not exist."

I started typing, "I write using a pseudonym" but then stopped, something within me believed adding to the lie would do no good.

Just tell him the truth. Just tell him you're useless, of no use to him, and the entire operation was some ruse to feel less alone.

Jiro said, "I want to trust you."

I couldn't do it. I couldn't tell him the truth. I was willing to sacrifice it all to shy away from my own deceit. I was a coward. I will always be a coward. So I told Jiro I did have notes. I really did have notes. That part, at least, was true.

"It hasn't really been edited down, but I have some writing here for the project."

Jiro texted, "Let me see."

"Do you want me to send to you via email or—"

"Here, paste it here, for me to read."

I sent him highly improvised versions of what would become the first two chapters of this book. In them lacked any verity in my motivations. Instead, it spoke of when we met.

We all wake up every day. In those first conscious moments is the most important act of all: the choice to align and continue. It is so much easier to walk away than to stick around and commit.

The day abandons you, the night consumes you.

When ten minutes passed, I texted, "Should I keep sending more?"

And then I received a paragraph-long text:

"From the heart. Routine is the structure. You walk within a routine and from there you must make the choice to pledge your hours. Awakening, the struggle you are writing about, is a concern. It defines a depression characteristic of a loss of purpose. Have you experienced this consistently, or are you writing from the objective, beckoning the entirety of the humanity? I enjoyed the last sentence. It adheres to a relatable feeling of being consumed by one's work. The devotion I have never lost. The devotion I aspire to hold like a wife."

I didn't know what to say.

"Send me more."

I pulled from another document, my attempt at making sense of that night.

The grand opening—

The crowd passed me over and soon I was at the end of the block, street corner staring nowhere in particular. I heard voices, or rather one, a man with a deep yet raspy tenor, the accent undeniable, but what careened over every chortle was the manner with which he spoke of, well, anything. The sincerity of each sentence caught me off guard. He spoke as though there was never a doubt what he said could be wrong, could be defeated and compromised by the opinions of others.

It wasn't like me to, without hesitation, strike up a conversation with a stranger. He wasn't the founder of the restaurant, nor was he a man of passion. Rather, he was like me, caught in the orbit of others. The difference is when someone looked through him, negating his very being, he looked right back and made sure to leave an impression, one you wouldn't soon forget.

This is how I first met Jiro.

I maintained my silence. If there were a clock in my room, I might have been driven mad by the ticking. Instead, I clicked around, one tab to the next, attempting to center myself and dupe the only person I couldn't dupe, myself, into thinking this wasn't a big deal.

My heart beating rapidly in my chest was verification of importance of Jiro's critique.

I identified a line that might have upset him:

He wasn't the founder of the restaurant, nor was he a man of passion. Rather, he was like me, caught in the orbit of others.

Why hadn't I deleted this line before sending?

Jiro replied with just the one word, "Wow."

"Are you okay with it?"

Jiro took it far better than expected, "Yes. It was impressive to bear witness to that night from your perspective. I understood you were shy, or upset. I hadn't understood you were able to read me as well as I had read you. There must be more to this scene. Please send."

Please send.

I was exhausted, emotionally this pulled me every which way, unsure of Jiro would find the next sentence, something I hadn't thought was incorrect, the one that sends him over the edge.

This could very well be instance of emotional manipulation, but he had much to say, which was all the evidence I needed to understand that I wasn't as clever a liar as I had expected. Perhaps Jiro knew more than he had originally led on.

Copy/paste, and I hit send, deciding to send it as-is, no edits, no erasure. Take no heed in the fact that I allowed myself to be so vulnerable in what was already a compromised situation, one where I countered being vulnerable by choosing to increase it. Textbook description of the word, "stubborn," because it had to be my choice to be so candid, not anyone else's.

Jiro asked me, "What are you doing here?" It was as if he already knew me. When I told him the truth, "I was passing through," he didn't find my answer to be acceptable. I had never been so intensely judged and yet, at the same time, compelled to continue being judged.

"What do you do?"

Not, *"Who are you?"* He never asked me for my name.

Rather it was—what do you do? What are you really worth?

And for that matter, are you worth my time?

Authenticity had more to do with reverence to the history of gastronomy than whether or not a chef mimicked the work of others. Authenticity was every bit a matter of maintaining the quality and deliciousness of a cuisine as it was a need to innovate wherever necessary.

"For this Kazuya hasn't the means."

Jiro's reply wasn't wholly unexpected: "This was your first impression of me?"

"Yeah," I said.

"I have been told by most that my demeanor is difficult to read. Your stance reveals a side of me that may very well exist yet I cannot remember being so judgmental. I was concerned for you. You carried the wavering heart of a person I know well."

My excuse: "It's how I saw it, which is what you told me you wanted."

"Much of my reluctance had to do with the way you looked."

"Wait," I hit send, and then added, "What?"

Could it be that Jiro was suddenly reaching for an apology?

Or was I reading into something that wasn't there?

"I saw in you a younger version of myself."

Jiro sent a line culled from my own: *"I had never been so intensely judged and yet, at the same time, compelled to continue being judged."*

He offered no other explanation.

Okay, fine, feeling frustrated, I went off the cuff, "That's the truth though, and in many ways, it should be considered a compliment. I did not feel negatively judged. It's kind of like what's happening right now actually. I'm showing part of me and in doing so, of course I'm going to be judged. But I am also feeling like you're taking it the wrong way."

I was full of shit, testing the waters, twisting the dagger deeper into the wound my writing had already opened.

Jiro responded with another line, quoted:

"To produce something from thin air is far more difficult than con-
ceiving of something that has already provided a narrative."

What did he want me to say? I texted back, "That's a line you said."

Jiro started typing, stopped, and then started again. I watched, feeling numb.

"Indeed. You rendered it so well. I had not remembered my words but you had not only done so but cast it in a convenient light. It was difficult to read, perhaps because it struck me as so attuned to the reality of the situation. I ask for no excuse. This is only reaction, nothing more."

I should have been relieved, "Thanks. I am only doing my best."

"A well-rendered scene."

The compliment that sent me over the deep end: "You are a great writer. I could not have conceived of such a scene in a seamless manner."

Immediate reaction: I could do better. It's not that good. I lost the point of the scene long before I finished it. The scene runs on too long. It doesn't run on long enough.

What I do say is, "That means a lot," and then I add, knowing well that I am absolutely doomed, "The more you give me, the more I'll be able to tell."

I received no reply.

Received 9:02PM. Three hours and two minutes since my last text.

"Thank you for finding interest in telling my story."

I was so screwed.

This is how I gain and lose a friend. This is how I attempt to put togeth-er the scraps, into a story that may doom me. Please. Go right ahead.

I hoped to achieve a fraction of my promise. It isn't penance. It's punishment, because no matter how much a person tried, I worried Jiro would not be around to read this.

LIGHT RAIN, LOST TIME

*H*e called me on a Thursday morning, so uncharacteristic because he preferred the silence and ease of a text message, more so because he had explicitly outlined in the rules there was to be no filming, no thought of the documentary, on weekdays. Everyone carries with them a mechanism to thwart how memory can suddenly capture you, stumbling into a space dark, yet so familiar, enough to steal away a new experience. Jiro must have viewed our every interaction as being pulled underground, returning to a tunnel where the details of his past had been buried, thought to be for good.

Jiro had a story to tell, and it begun with the words "Brooklyn" and "bridge," and ended with phrases "light rain" and "lost time."

I picked up by the third ring. You bet I ditched my plan of staring at my laptop screen, writing about not being able to get to the root of what I was trying to write about in favor of meeting Jiro, the Brooklyn Bridge in the rain.

The cloudy skies threatening downpour, I walked the bridge looking for a familiar face.

He had told me not to bring the camera but I did anyway, making sure to take the waterproof shell with me. I must have looked like a professional, forced to carry it in my hands due to the bulkiness of the shell, the spare few that walked the bridge too giving me curious looks.

Perhaps it was more to do with how I had been far more aware of myself, as if I were on this bridge with no intent of leaving it. Certainly, I have been suicidal. More than ideation, I had walked a ledge, so to speak, and dabbled with the thought that I could choose my last thoughts, actions, the fate of my boring little life. What kept me from jumping wasn't pity or someone coming to my rescue, but rather the thought that my mediocrity extended into the work I had written. I couldn't even escape in a thrilling, well-conceived piece of fiction. How pitiful. And so, I didn't jump.

To kill yourself, you had to leave behind something of worth or else you're just another dot fading in the distance.

I found Jiro somewhere in the middle of the bridge, hands in his coat, shivering slightly, the rain beginning to drizzle. The sky darkened and I remember walking up, already filming, beckoned by the dramatic lighting, the understanding that "This is it!" This was what I had asked of Jiro all along: show me something more than the telling of other's poor culinary travails.

Show me why.

Though I don't have the question, please, give me all the answers.

Jiro pointed his attention to the water below, never looking at me, not even when I confided in him about having attempted the same, the same dive. Approaching Jiro, I took a position to his right. Sensing that it was me, Jiro spoke of the first time he walked this bridge.

"I had preferred the Manhattan Bridge to Brooklyn, but it was ill-equipped for what I needed to do." Though he never explicitly said the word, "suicide," he gave me the necessary details, the cues necessary to make the connection.

"I didn't ask you to bring the camera," Jiro cleared his throat, wiping the fresh drizzle from his forehead.

Apologizing, feeling frustrated for being forever at the whim of Jiro's demands, I defended the filming, "This is how we'll be able to tell your story: by getting footage whenever we can."

"An individual's failure to give into death," Jiro said dispassionately, "shall it function to be the crux of my story? If so, I should step up onto this ledge and allow you to film it."

This is where someone says something like "Don't be so dramatic" or "You are worth so much more," but instead I said nothing. Silence washed over us and Jiro, lowering his voice, the passion that had always been identifiable now missing, spoke of his first week in America.

He had been homeless, living alternatively across a half dozen different subway stations; whenever possible, he tempted one of the parks, but he claimed, "They set the homeless on fire, bleeding them out for entertainment."

The danger of finding comfort, he had been lucky to have familiarity with the English language, though his ability to speak took much longer. I remembered listening and getting excited—I was finally getting the story, the real story—and every change in angle, every slight movement made for the sake of getting a better cinematic shot, was done with the utmost care.

That rainy afternoon, on the bridge, he didn't tell me the truth. He didn't go so far as to even explain what led him to wanting to jump. Instead, he spoke of what it was like to know, seeped to the very core of your being, to have signed off on the inevitable.

"The bridge was no more. The pain of each step had disappeared. I walked on rainclouds. Like today, I was drenched, shivering and cold. The world around me reflected every feeling, every feeling I did not have, for I felt nothing. I was at peace. All that was left to be done was the step up and the step back down, the drop would be, I had imagined, the bliss ongoing forever."

I have that on film. I have transcribed it. I feel bad that I haven't a clue where to place it in relation to the rest of the footage. That after-

55

noon, the would-be scene, was set aside, full enough to be part of the feature, yet something in the telling leads me to believe I don't have the right, and neither does anyone else, to impart this in any other manner than verbatim.

Jiro would have jumped, but something tethered him to consciousness. He stepped back down, walked to a shelter, and ate his first meal in two days.

"All throughout, I was at peace," he said. "In the morning, the bitter aftertaste of the miserable meal I had eaten lingering, I tasted what could be tragedy. It gave me the passion I had lost to treat tragedy with triumph. The flavors I imagined to be true, I dreamed them to be real. That morning, I understood that they were—real. They were real, waiting for someone to understand their place."

Silence fell upon us.

I watched Jiro stare out onto the sea. The drizzle became a steady rain. Imagine lightning and thunder and treacherous winds, if you like. Actually, I would prefer it to be that way. It rained in that steady manner, the sort that tells you it will last all day, no beginning and no end.

Soaking wet and still, the camera pointed in his direction, I broke the silence and said, "Sad classical music intensifies." Maybe not the most considerate thing to say.

"Sorry, bad joke," I said.

He asked me if I tried.

I could have said so many different things, I could have told him the truth.

In the fiction, I threw up the partially digested pills and attempted to cover up the entire thing, but the following afternoon my partner (because I might as well be dating someone in this fiction, god knows it's been almost a year since I have gone on a date) dropped by my apartment and the smell, yeah, you could say she smelled it from a mile away. The odor of bile and stomach acids, of chemicals decomposed, it gave it all away. The fiction ends with, "I ended up in therapy."

Note to self: I probably need therapy.

The rain worsened, making it more difficult to see into the distance.

I cracked another joke, equally bad—so bad I can no longer remember what it was, something about comedians being the saddest artists of all.

Jiro's reply: "I feel empty watching comedies."

We were the only two on the bridge.

I said I preferred standup. "It feels more... honest."

"It is only in seeing the emptiness of others that I am able to laugh."

I thought about then said, "The emptiness is relatable."

Jiro nodded, "There is humor in understanding we have survived it. In surviving it we are able to laugh and celebrate our survival."

Our clothes were plastered to our skin; my hair caked to the sides of my head, bangs hiding half of my face. The beads of rain rolled down Jiro's bald head, causing him to squint, blink rapidly, and occasionally cover his face to keep from harming his eyes.

"Might this be the sort of content that makes for a better story?"

"Yes," I turned off the camera. "I want to know about the sushi you created. I want to know about your work."

Return to where it all started, or at least where we started: Kazuya's grandiose restaurant. Much to my surprise, there wasn't a line, no wait during peak hours, the dinner crowd nonexistent. I was led to one of the back booths, as requested, demanding the privacy of being unseen by others, especially if Jiro had somehow decided to dine here too.

I covered all my tracks, retraced and reviewed all that had occurred. I lied to the server, saying I was a writer, a journalist, sure why not? I inquired whether Kazuya himself were available for an interview. Not only was he available that evening, mere mention of writing for the New York

Times (if you haven't already surmised, I am an excellent liar, the kind that dresses for the occasion, able to be so authentic to the fiction spun around each endeavor because I, too, and spun by the circumstances to follow) resulted in a comped meal (I could get used to this).

"The house's specialty," the server had said, presenting a sampler of sushi. Much to my delight, this wasn't sashimi; rather, it was something special, a fusion of different cuisines, the sort of thing that would have disgusted Jiro, but that night, I liked that it would have done so. I adored the fact that I was in enemy territory, and moreover, I was deceiving the enemy in the same manner, and with the same precision, as I had Jiro.

Underneath the charade, I was miserable. To recognize just how deficient you are, as a person, yeah, it's a very special sort of shame. The sort that takes every ounce of energy to hide as you interview the enemy.

Watch how easy it is for me to befriend and flatter a person:

"What is this," pointing to the third piece of sushi on the plate, "such a compelling design. It excites me into thinking about what it might taste like."

Kazuya grinned, "Why not see how it tastes?"

The sushi devoured, you could say I was stunned. It was good. Better than good. It was great. I wanted to try more. Never mind Kazuya continuing to make (intentionally) sexual references to the taste and temptation of "his sushi."

I catered to his ego: "So, if I wanted to order even more, would that be a problem?"

Signaling to the server, he said, "You are insatiable."

Me: "One need be to understand the true depth of complex flavors."

(Wow, talk about believing one's own bullshit.)

Kazuya sat there, fixed, judging my every move, as I ate, clearly getting off on my evident adoration for his creation. I imagined the same for anyone that labored over the impossibility of their demands, for every creator demanded something from their craft that might never be clear, never be unearthed from the years, decades really, of work.

But this Kazuya had achieved something great: He created a menu, a wide range of sushi that countered tradition. He created his *own* tradition.

The interview consisted of questions like, "What do you think determines the difference between 'delicious' and 'disgust?'" and another, "How do you balance flavors?" The more Kazuya spoke, the less I understood, but sure, I pretended to write down his replies, claiming my phone placed screen-up, on the table was set to record every word.

It took the full three-course meal, sushi, followed by more sushi, followed by an entrée, in this case, a fusion of tempura and barbeque, followed by a dessert, fried ice cream, again all fronted by Kazuya (why must it be so easy to live a lie?), to get to the heart of my inquiry.

I wanted to bring up Jiro's name. I hoped that hearing word of Jiro would register in Kazuya something that would corroborate what I hoped to be true all along.

Sure, between all the talk and banter, I never shook free the doubt that Jiro may very well have gone silent because he doubted me, or worse: His online sleuthing led him to one of the far corners of the internet where my writing existed, unread but otherwise still enough evidence of my role, as a fraud. I had plagiarized another writer's work, and was caught.

Changing your name didn't change the very core of your being. The trick is to hide in the open, never denying a claim but instead turning the doubt, the accusation, on the accuser. Much like how Kazuya reacted when I brought up Jiro.

It wasn't fear. It wasn't praise.

Kazuya choked, "Now that's a sorry-ass sight to behold."

What? Yeah, I got a little angry. I said some things, which upset Kazuya. He remained visibly calm but I could hear it in his voice as he defended his work, his restaurant, while I repeated what Jiro had said. Kazuya put two and two together, "You shouldn't trust someone that lives in the shadows of others. They want nothing more than to switch places. They want the light as much as anyone else."

"Jiro is a genius," I said, feeling personally attacked, and so I attacked the meal, claiming he doused everything in that spicy mayo, that all he really did was bastardize other traditions.

Kazuya laughed, "I see his influence has outweighed logic."

Again, I had to ask him what (the fuck) he meant.

The proclamation was simple, yet everything I feared: Yes, he knew Jiro, not just knew of him but rather knew him well enough to disclose Jiro's age, 91, and his suicide attempt, jumping off the Brooklyn Bridge. How could he have been so privy to that information?

How could he have known about the suicide attempt?

"How could you not know?" Kazuya held back laughter, "The poor bastard tells everyone of his struggle, his sacrifice for 'his art.' He insults your work and then says he envisions much better. But where is Jiro's sushi? Where can I try the so-called perfect otoro?"

Visualize a person so struck by what was said, his bottom lip visibly quivers. He is speechless and after hearing what Kazuya says next, tears well up and dribble down, a silent cry, the sort you normally wipe away before anyone can notice.

But Kazuya notices, and then he gets his servers to notice:

"The old man is toxic. The city knows of its failures, and it keeps tabs on every single one. We let old Jiro complain. He is a reminder for every chef in the city—we need to work hard so that never, we will *never*, be like Jiro."

The tears, and then the biggest insult:

"But it seems you're well on your way, Jiro."

The server placed the bill in front of me. Kazuya and I exchanged a glance. You've got to be fucking kidding me. I slammed down the credit card, looking away as the server disappeared with it. Kazuya stood from the booth, cracked his knuckles, and then left me without another word.

I shut my eyes, repeating the words, 'This isn't happening."

A tap on the table got my attention. It was the server.

"The card was declined."

Of course. I retrieved it and then fumbled for an excuse, "Let me call my bank." The server wouldn't leave my side as I wandered down one of the back halls, with nobody to call, doing what I did best, pretending there was this whole thing, identity theft and blah blah blah, whatever, until finally I handed over my debit card, which would work because I had money in there, enough to cover this bill but not the subway ride home.

Good riddance, I'm out the door.

You can't leave such an embarrassing situation without leaving part of yourself.

And then he called—just like that. Must have been over three weeks without so much as a text message. Jiro sounded like nothing happened, picking up where we left off like it was completely okay. He invited me to go for a walk in "his neighborhood." I hid my true feelings and agreed to meet at 3PM off the Flushing JMZ. Jiro waited for me near the steps leading down from the raised platform. He acted different that day, far more willing to express himself, giving me a tour of his neighborhood. When we reached a five-story walkup, the stoop cracked and ruptured in random places, a building that had seen better days, I asked, "So this is where you live?"

"Yes," said Jiro, sitting down on the second step.

I remained standing and looking up at the front door, "We're not going inside?"

Had I suddenly gained confidence? No, just frustrated, my patience worn thin.

The camera in my right hand, I sighed, "Look, I'm not about to waste my time..."

I was frustrated. This building might not actually be where he lived. "How can I believe you? How can *the viewer* believe you? If you aren't honest with me, we could really say anything and it wouldn't matter. People would believe what they want, or worse: They wouldn't care at all."

I told him the viewer had even less patience than me, and Jiro got quiet.

A typical humid afternoon in Brooklyn, I was witness, and worse, the culprit, of seeing an old man break down. If I was to unearth any truth, I had to make a move. Now was the time.

There were no tears, not even a single whimper. Jiro sat there, head in his hands, shielded from view. I stood facing the stoop where he sat, recording the entire confession.

I said more things, mostly to make him feel even worse, because I wanted him to be upset. I wanted him to be as upset as I still was that night at Kazuya's. Dammit, I spent $131 on that meal! Come clean, Jiro, come clean!

"Speak up. For the camera!"

He coughed, "I fled."

"You fled."

"I fled my homeland. I have fled every place I once called home."

Jiro claimed he had a bad breakup—gave into the embarrassment and depression of a dire end to a five-year commitment. "I had given myself to my work, but then someone entered my life and gave herself to my life, supporting my passion so much that she became the reason for my passion. My passion had much to do with the life I no longer called my own."

She left him for someone else. So he fled. Maybe not the most logical thing to do, but when you're that low, nothing you do is logical.

Jiro couldn't look me in the eye. All throughout the telling, he was a broken mess without the actual cleanup. There were no tears, no visible discomfort.

Jiro, you would have to do better than that.

I brought the camera in closer, and with perhaps as much confidence as I will ever muster, I challenged him, "That's a lie and you know it."

There he was, face no longer hidden behind cold hands. He looked right at the camera and said, "How could you know?"

Because I'm a liar too, Jiro.

"Because I know you."

How to kick someone when they're already down in five steps or less.

"The Jiro I know wouldn't let a broken heart ruin the very thing that gave him heart in the first place." I mentioned Kazuya's name. Sadness, homelessness, alcoholism, manic depression: I pointed to every rupture, and then I did one better and said that you might have fled, "But it wasn't because you were being hunted. It wasn't because someone stole your heart. You fled all on your own, and I need to know why. If this is going to be a documentary. No—if this is going to be the very thing you want, *your story,* well, you need to tell the real story."

Jiro, prove me wrong.

This city is wrong. You are better than this.

"Just come clean, Jiro, it's okay."

Enough was enough—he told me to turn around. Not to look at him.

"The camera needs to—"

"So be it," Jiro shouted, "but don't look at me."

I took heed in this demand, and slowly but surely, as I watched people walk down the sidewalk, oblivious to the drama that had consumed his life and mine. Look at their faces: I wondered how many people find worth in something outside of themselves.

Thankfully, I understood. Perhaps nobody else ever would.

Perhaps this is why the camera keeps rolling, long after he confesses everything. Perhaps this is why I sit down next to him, the both of us in frame, viewable and like two broken individuals, sitting and wondering where it all went wrong.

63

This is the only footage I have of us, in frame. Every other piece one of us is off camera, or partially hidden for reasons that have more so to do with my own inexperience. Perhaps this is why I won't be able to accept his admission and it will eat me alive.

I walked the city by night. I walked the city looking for my own losses, the places I used to visit, many of them no longer open for business.

I walked the city hoping someone would out me as an imposter, claiming to be the real me, and like out of some sci-fi flick, I would melt, a half-being posing in full, and then the real me meets Jiro at a restaurant within walking distance, a table for two, Jiro sitting there the real story all written out for me, ready for to be read.

I walked the city trying to forget that it was now my turn to come clean.

What happened to Jiro?

He ran away because his own son stole from him, not merely a recipe but more so an entire passion, stolen. Your own child stealing your life away from you. Gone, and the success to follow you watch from a nearby corner, battling a lose-lose situation: Destroy your son or destroy yourself?

Your life, as you knew it and had worked tirelessly to define, completely over.

The rest of the story writes itself. It isn't glamorous and it is why few will ever know what Jiro went through. Except for another fraud. You don't take offers from strangers unless you are looking to be found out. No. If I'm going to be honest, I just wanted to do something for him, before the truth, my own confession, would take it all away.

WHAT KEEPS YOU ALIVE

*I*woke up at my desk. It must have been around 2AM. Nothing new or special about falling asleep at my desk. That's not the point. I stared straight at the darkened screen of my laptop, my fingers still on the keyboard. Rereading the last sentence, I wrote, it was all I could think about.

"This is going to kill the guy."

The truth sets you free.

I deleted the sentence and went back to sleep.

"What are you doing right now?"

I should have said, "Halfway to a sort of self-proposed madness."

I had spent the time alternating between feeling sorry for myself and reading about famous authors like J.D. Salinger and directors like Sofia Coppola on Wikipedia, more living vicariously on my part. I should have said, "Feeling sad."

Instead I went with, "Wasting my life."

Jiro's side of the line went quiet.

"What's up?" I said, feeling better. Jiro had pulled me away from my thoughts.

"I had some thoughts about the documentary."

The abruptness always caught my breath. I suppressed a cough, "Oh... yeah?" A whole list of possible complaints ran through my mind, culminating with something along the lines of "you are just as big a liar as me."

Jiro asked me again about what I had said (what did I say? I can't remember), "When we had filmed on the Bridge, you spoke of desiring to know my work."

I remembered. How could I have forgotten?

Jiro's voice became clearer, more confident, "I have designed and cultivated an entire seasonal omakase menu, to which I practice whenever possible."

"You actually make the sushi?"

"Yes, I feel so lucky when I get to practice."

There was the trademark passion in his voice, right on schedule. He had been so defeated, so downtrodden in the days after his confession. Our routine broke, and now the only interaction I had with Jiro was via phone call at random, always Jiro the one that called, not me. He called from a handful of different phone numbers, but the only one I recognized was the one he gave me first.

I started writing down notes in Word.

"Where do you practice?"

"In the minutes and moments where I can center myself," said Jiro.

Sign of a director, the would-be writer cutting in, "Jiro, I need details. If this is going to work, we need direct, concrete details."

"Garrett graciously allows me to practice before and after closing at the restaurant."

"So you practice at Benihana?"

No reply. I couldn't bear to conjure the picture of Jiro practicing at the sushi bar, using what must have been inferior cuts of meat, the

66

sushi he laboriously cut and made, he couldn't have possibly had the time to prepare and so he did the best he could by making sushi no one would ever eat. I asked him if he taste-tested the sushi.

"No," Jiro's voice faded, making what he said next almost indecipherable.

"I didn't get that. Jiro, could you repeat it? You cut out for a bit."

The telling, it was every bit of what I feared. "...I cannot stomach the ingredients, they purchase their tuna, for instance, from a vendor I have taken to be not at all interested in providing delectable tuna but rather providing as much business with maximum profit possible."

I interrupted, "Is this why you couldn't even look the other chefs in the eye?"

Again, he didn't say, which provided more of an explanation than any statement. Switching topics, I settled not on the dissolution of our routine and "production" and instead on Jiro's own wellbeing. Shocking to think we seldom talked about our own moods. There was so much to be gained from explaining to others, and coincidentally yourself, the things that bother you.

I started by example, "When you called I was upset, really on the verge of tears. But it was nice to have you call. We haven't really talked the way we used to quite a bit. We haven't been working on the documentary, you know."

"Yes," Jiro solemnly said, "I haven't been well. It pained me to tell you, for I haven't told anyone the truth of my own betrayal, my cowardice. I ran away from a life at the pristine moment where I faced an important trial. I was given a trial and instead of challenging it, I fled. I fled not only a life but myself. This is quite a lot to take in, and I should apologize."

"No," I countered, "you can't take back what already happened and so there's no need to apologize. At least to me. I completely understand. Life doesn't usually play itself out the way a person imagined it."

Look at me, preaching like I am somehow excluded from this.

Jiro seemed to ease off the concern, even trying to tell a joke.

"When you look at a sushi roll, what do you see?"

This was where I said, "I don't know."

"I just seafood."

I faked a laugh, which Jiro didn't buy, and then I had the idea:

"What the documentary is missing is everything about what makes you a genius. Why not skip the interviews and go right to the dining experience? Let's make it happen, Jiro. I really think this is the best way to present the film."

Confused, Jiro fumbled for something to say, "Have we not already been discussing this?"

"No—and we don't have to disclose the past. We can come up with a different angle. I think the entirety of this documentary should be the actual procuring of ingredients, creation, and dining of your menu. I want to give you that spotlight."

I thought about it and then added, "I want to get the attention of viewers the way you got my attention seemingly so long ago, at that grand opening."

Silence on the other line.

I added, "I want people to know what they're missing."

Still silent, I continued, building up momentum, doing my best to express my enthusiasm, because I really wanted to do this.

"We could go to the fish market, really spend the way you liked, getting the fish and ingredients that meet your expectations, and we can film you prepping and cooking. It makes so much sense the more I think about it. Enough of the mess surrounding everything—let's focus on your craft. Let's focus on what keeps you alive."

He must have heard it in my voice, the enthusiasm, because with little more than a "yes" we were back on track. Our routine became a daily scouring the city, walking much like I used to, but this time Jiro walked with to me. We looked, and I mean really looked, at menus everywhere with an objective eye. We hunted for what we needed to make this a true dining experience. This was how I met Jiro again, walking together out of the shadows and into the bright light of film production. It all seemed so possible: Jiro's passion bled into every detail discussed. And me? I was inspired. I could see the script, scene-for-scene, how this documentary, and more so our friendship, would play out. If I chose to peer off into the distance, I could see the entire duration running its course. A month or so of nonstop chatting with Jiro about sushi, learning and I mean really learning, about both sushi and how to produce a film.

Echoing throughout those days were, shockingly, my own words, rather than Jiro's:

Let's focus on what keeps you alive. This was what everyone calls "the good times," that parcel of time and memory where things are going right, nothing at all could go wrong.

I am as excited writing about it as I was living through it. It couldn't have lasted, but I can already see the temptation to sabotage this section, slowing down the writing process, so that I live, forever, in these memories, forever in the writing and rewriting of these moments.

A writer can write themselves into a corner without too much trouble; if you do, might as well write yourself into a corner with a cradle.

Transcripts from a sushi-dining experience:

"There are three cuts of tuna—akami, chutoro, and otoro. Akami is lean cut, a subtle flavor, and infinitely more sophisticated. A long time ago, when preservation wasn't adequate, the fatty sections of the tuna were tossed and the lean cuts were preserved in casks of soy sauce. Tuna, when combined with soy, creates a savory, pinnacle

match. This can very well be the peak of masterful sushi. Chutoro is the medium cut tuna, aged to bring out its essential flavors, and otoro is the thicker, fattier cut, and it is important for it to be as fla-grant as it is fatty. It is essential for it to melt in your mouth. Otoro is quite popular, and is well received and preferred by many customers. Typically, the tuna itself is aged a few days. Some do so for two days, others five, some give it only a day. I have always preferred to let it marinate for three. The bigger fish can go up to ten days It all depends on the quality of the tuna.

"The essence of a masterfully prepared piece of tuna is in umami. When you eat the tuna together with vinegared rice and soy sauce, the sense of euphoria essential to umami is unlocked. Each tuna carries its own taste. No two tuna are identical. I have always found it glamorous to see such a unique difference separating each cut of tuna.

"If you work at a sushi restaurant, tuna is your mainstay. It must be present in the course, the menu. You can substitute and customize your omakase menu but tuna must be at the crux of your offering. If not, you might as well keep the doors closed. Opening for business will only lead to poor ratings, disappointment, and perhaps the destruction of your restaurant. For many reasons, tuna is the most popular sushi topping today."

"Could you see a future where tuna is no longer as popular?"

Jiro looked around the restaurant, which wasn't his, and more-over, where we technically should never be allowed, especially after hours, but thanks to Garrett, the fantasy would outlast nearly every doubt and deception. Our defiance was soft, less a statement and more a simulacrum.

We used what Benihana had in terms of ingredients. Every single cut of meat Jiro used, every pound of rice prepared for practice, was written off as pity.

Garrett did all he could to hide the discrepancies. I wonder, even now, if any of this got back to corporate.

"I don't think so," said Jiro, as he cut the tuna.

I quieted down and filmed as he gently pressed one palm against the slab of tuna, the other hand carrying the knife, blade so sharp, dampened by water for ease of cutting, glistened under the otherwise washed out fluorescent light. We were the lone two in the back kitchen, where any glamor was undone for the sake of cleanliness and efficiency—steel, linoleum, and marble. The blade cut right through the tuna so swiftly, I imagined it doing the same with human muscle. Right through, the blade would not even slow upon reaching bone.

Jiro held a thin slice of tuna, "Akami," for the camera.

This was night one of many, and the first in a series of marathon sessions where Jiro became star, intern, stagehand, and promoter all in one. I became director, writer, producer. We understood each other's needs. I could tell when Jiro wanted to stop, turn the camera off, and take a break. He understood when I wasn't understanding the angle, the instruction, and he would always trail off and say, "Perhaps this is the street we had imagined."

Jiro cut another slice. I instructed him to cut and care to each "as if I weren't here, and you were doing this all by yourself."

"One never does this entirely by themselves. The food has to be enjoyed by another."

"Say that into the camera," I tapped the side of my face, instructing to look ever so slightly to the right of the camera, providing a more flattering angle, "and details. More details."

Jiro cut another lean slice, adjusted his gaze, and enunciated each word clearly, "Food is never a lonely experience. You are not merely consuming nutrients; you are experiencing its flavors and creating memories. This experience is shared with the food you meet."

Soon the cut of tuna has been tended to and we have over two dozen strips of akami. Jiro turned his attention to another task, the act of cleaning every surface and item used, as he specified in clear detail how easy it is to poison a flavor with something as "seemingly harmless a messy cooking space."

I joked about the cleanliness of this kitchen, and he looked calmly into the camera, "Half of a chef's job isn't cooking; it is the painstaking task of preparation and purification of the spaces that complement the culinary experience."

I nodded and grinned, a perfect take. The timestamp on the camera rolling by was an ever-present reminder that everything is temporary.

Holding up a bottle of Kikkoman soy sauce, Jiro winked, "This segment is brought to you by Kikkoman." Tapping the label of the bottle, he tried not to crack up, "specifically this bottle of Kikkoman, the original, which I imagine must be as decrepit as me."

The camera caught it all, every slip and stutter, even the part where he turned to me and asked, "Do they even do this anymore? Live sponsorships? Should it now be automatic, or rather automated?" And then me, off camera, could be heard saying, "I don't fucking know."

Then Jiro giving me a hard time, "You know oh so little, therefore we need to stuff you with sushi. Stuff you with understanding. There must be something in that skull of yours."

Crack it open with a mallet, find out if I'm anything at all you imagined.

In these moments, I never stopped recording, as if these glimpses were of a person Jiro had long since let go, burned and buried by the pressures of satisfying his demons.

Camera right in my face, blurry and off frame, he asked, "If you became happy, would you have less to write about? If you became happy, would you have more to write about?"

Without thinking, I posed a third, "If I were a writer, would I be happy?"

"You should know," Jiro chuckled, "the life of a writer is the one you are living."

Or so you think.

"You are right, you are right." Believe your own lies. "You have to figure that in all those long hours fighting for the right language, you find a few synonyms for happiness. That way, even if you're miserable, with the drop of a synonym, you don't even have to know."

"Might you have a few synonyms on hand?" Jiro asked.

"Do you have the booze ready?"

Jiro reached under one of the counters, retrieving our liquor of choice. "This sake is for paying customers. But a synonym or three shall suffice."

The things we do to blur our consciousness.

Look at me, and who I am: The very thing that eludes me is myself.

Content.

Satisfied.

Pleased.

Jovial.

Chill.

Cheerful.

Exuberant.

Merry (not one of my favorites. It increases the happy in happiness rather than muting and muddying it).

Excited.

Jolly (ugh).

Passionate (probably the one I use the most).

Thrilled.

Motivated.

Can't complain.

Jiro added another—*"umami."*

To which all I had was, "Sure, sure, just pass the sake."

RANDOM ACTS OF RESPECT

W hat are we working on tonight?"

"Halibut. We have been lucky enough that there is plenty of halibut here left from today, so I will not let this go to waste. We will have to prepare this quickly. But it is my hope that the footage you gain from this will be worth the hasty nature of preparation."

I prompted for a little more, "Are you comfortable with compromise?"

Jiro placed both hands on the cool surface of the counter, "I am not. However, I have need to compromise, right? We might be running low on time."

This was news to me. "Any particular reason?"

Jiro made a face. "The halibut. It will soon be useless to us."

"Oh."

Once again, my imposter syndrome blurring the line between logic and the lingering truth.

"Halibut is very popular, though naturally no comparison with tuna. There should be no thought of comparing the two, for halibut has a very different taste. It is light, delectable, and delicate. You can prepare it several different ways, but I have preferred to age it five or six hours, chilling it, and the simplicity of a diluted soy marinade, with the slightest pinch of sugar added to the soy. By the looks of it, the age of our halibut is just right."

"That's good," I said, not expecting that we would be eating the food. In our previous session, we got drunk and forgot to eat any more than a couple pieces of the tuna. Imagine the worst hangover possible and then turn up the intensity to eleven.

"Keep talking," I instructed, wandering around the kitchen, each step taken carefully to keep as close a shot of Jiro as possible. He continued preparing the sushi, each thin slice of halibut having already been cut before I arrived, and I captured some excellent footage of the rice being added to the topping, the delicate rhythms of each press, zooming in on Jiro's hands as he placed two fingers against the fold of the piece, doing it again a few times, the swiftness of each motion appeared so effortless you understood how much practice went into achieving that balance.

Rapt by the rhythm of each press, I watched, once piece after the other, Jiro combining the rice, the wasabi, the halibut topping, and merged them into one, something so seemingly simple and yet with the various hand motions and presses, he performed a culinary magic trick.

During one of our drunken chats late at night, after filming ceased, he would let me try and fail miserably. We would both laugh because we were drunk, always drunk, and I just did the stupidest thing I could ever do, without realizing it.

I tried to mimic it but the first attempt I crushed the rice, flattening it enough that it lost the correct shape. My second attempt, the topping slipped off the rice and though I retrieved it, even after it fell to the floor, laughing hysterically while saying, "Hold up, hold up, it's just a little dirty, it's still good, it's still good!"

The third attempt, I pressed them all together and it sort of looked like a piece of sushi, except when I tried to brush the soy onto the top and it slipped out of my hands.

"Bon appetite!"

More laughter.

Looking back, I cherish these stupid moments. Jiro was so happy.

That night preparing halibut sushi, we spent upwards of three hours filming Jiro performing that technique of making the sushi. By the conclusion of it, his hands must have been brittle and sore.

I asked him, "How are your wrists, your fingers?"

Jiro retained that calm and collected demeanor, "They have never felt better. They missed the cool touch of sushi."

"How long since you've made sushi?"

Jiro offered a piece of halibut. I took it in, the flavors landing on my tongue in such a wondrously complex array that I couldn't process any of it.

I couldn't speak. Jiro did all the talking,

"It has been over a decade. I practice three times a week, the sushi prepared is either mine to eat or Garrett's, though the sushi I have created often goes refrigerated here at the restaurant. I couldn't possibly take the food with me. It was never mine to begin with."

I must have looked the part. Jiro clapped his hands together, "The sushi is sufficient?"

"I'm speechless," I said.

"Halibut has such a delicate taste, it can often translate to speechlessness—the human tastebuds can parse each flavor, though it can be quite difficult to ascertain beyond the rush that develops upon devouring. It requires a very delicate palate to identify each of its individual flavors."

I washed it down with some sake.

Jiro asked to be poured some too, "I was not aware that our filming was complete."

I shrugged, "We still need to film the tasting of the sushi."

To this he would consistently refuse. He would not allow me to film him eating his own sushi. Likewise, he preferred that I be also omitted. When pressed for more, he claimed, "If this is going to be intimate, I cannot be incestuous. Would you be proud spotted indulgently viewing and reading your work in public?"

"To be honest," I mused, "yes, I would, as a matter of pride."

He shook his head, drank, "It is not pride. It is being prejudiced. You taste behind the scenes; you should know what it feels like, tastes like, before it ever reaches the hands of others."

Jiro returned to the halibut. He turned away from the camera and ate a piece of sushi. "The earthy tone of this fish, it can dissuade others. I prepare it using a modest amount of soy marinade blazed with chili pepper and scallion hidden and blended with the wasabi."

We sat down at the counter, approximately 38 pieces of sushi between the both of us, 39 if you counted the one Jiro just ate. I turned the camera off, agreeing to his request. It might be a manner of opinion, sure, but I do not agree. But then, as I reflect on it now, I come to one conclusion. The artist does not seek only the satisfaction of popularity and praise from others. The artist seeks mastery of their craft. I sound like a tool, like I have been brainwashed by Jiro, by the artist gaze and all its obsession about mantra, ideal, and purpose. I stand by the belief that we do it to gain the respect of others. We make sacrifices to one day be the reason why someone else makes a sacrifice. Inspired by you, and/or your work, or perhaps inspired by the very nature of adoration, they vow upon your name that they will do the same, or die trying.

I guess I want nothing more than the satisfaction of being considered a success. When you live in the negative, unable to have anything to show for years of work, you become selfish. You have something to prove, which makes you see less of what's around you and more of what is ahead.

But as we ate and drank, a deafening silence fell upon the meal as we debated upon our motivations. Are we ever truly selfless?

"I desire to make great sushi," Jiro said, when I asked him about his ulterior motives.

"You don't want praise from others?"

He refused praise, claiming the praise he desired was from seeing people enjoy the meal.

"But don't you want to be remembered?"

He shook his head, "No."

"Then what is the point of this documentary? If you want to be known you also want to be remembered. I doubt you are much for the 15 minutes of fame variety."

Jiro didn't want to talk about it. "Such thoughts are toxic. Wrong intentions, you can taste it in the sushi you make. People get sick, they find something about it off-putting. Many chefs close their enterprise shortly after a level of fame due to the indulgence clouding their ability to understand their work."

"I guess I just hoped you believed in being something more."

Jiro refilled my glass, "You must focus on one thing at a time. You're nowhere near ready."

You know that feeling you have when everything around you changes color, everything becoming bolder while the volume is turned down low enough that all you can hear is your heartbeat, feel your palms sweating, all you can think about is how small and insignificant you are, how confused and wrong, the very thing that centered you pulled out from under you?

But we kept on with the conversation, soon discussing the body, and how it aches with time. Jiro spoke of the human liver, how resilient it is, capable of taking on so many toxins yet it continues, even as it dies, hardens, eventually giving in like anything else.

"But still we drink." He raised a glass. We laughed.

Another night of filming, one I wouldn't have traded for any price.

"And what about tonight, Jiro?"

"Tonight, we have," he paused, facing disappearing into the fridge, "mackerel!"

Yeah, we had already been drinking that night. Jiro and I had met at a bar five blocks from the restaurant to chat, initially, about how I envisioned the general structure of the documentary to fall into place. I texted a bunch of hype, claiming a eureka moment had occurred, but by the time we met at the bar, I had already told him everything via text.

I wanted it to be three movements—

The first movement is all memory, a primer, backstory—story of Jiro, of how sushi rose to prominence—as told from Jiro's own words.

The second movement is acumen, all about his sushi, mapped around the idea of delivering an entire omakase menu.

The third movement is present day, where Jiro has ended up. I require of him the confession and a series of revelations that speak of how he ended up working at Benihana, semi-homeless, unable to see past the day's worries.

The documentary ends with no catharsis, just Jiro about to exit the kitchen, readying to prepare a teppanyaki meal.

To my surprise, he agreed with the vulnerability—so we drank in celebration of holding nothing back, and then we went to the restaurant to film more sushi preparation and—"Mackerel, to be specific, umm, aji, or horse mackerel, shima-aji or striped mackerel, and ahh, what was the third?" Jiro stared blankly at the knife in his hand.

How much did he have to drink?

"The mackerel is a shiny fish," Jiro trailed off.

I burst out into laughter.

Jiro started laughing too. He slumped over the counter and said, "Ah, this is no good." He set down the knife, and I watched as it hit the counter at the wrong angle, making a tinny sound as it fell to the floor.

Jiro made no move to pick it back up.

I remained behind the camera, one arm leaning on a nearby storage crate and the other hanging limp at my side.

Jiro started up again, *"Mackerel spoils the quickest. If not tended to immediately, it will be ruined.* The same could be said for my wife. I never thought I would remarry here in America but I did. She needed be tended to immediately. You could not beckon her to wait until you got home, or to finish an important task; if she had something on her mind, a need, it was paramount that you cater to satisfying or fixing whatever it was she wanted. She was delicate. She never knew me."

Transcripts from a sushi-dining experience?

"You prepare the fish, the umm, the mackerel with salt. You cure it for four hours and then you wash it with vinegar."

Jiro reached for something, perhaps the knife, but nothing was there.

He folded his hands across his chest, "Oh, I may be a little drunk. We have not eaten dinner. I must prepare this sushi. Are you filming?"

He didn't move and I didn't say anything.

"You need to take some time, do not salt the wound as they say. You mustn't be so careless in your trauma. The bad will forever be bad if you salt it with the quick deception of getting better after a few days. I have not healed fully from even the loss of my father and my mother. My parents, I don't know them. I never have—my father liked to drink. He was making good money for a time but then it all fell apart. He salted his wounds by drowning in booze. He wouldn't let go of the past. I had nowhere to go. The place that was to be my home I discovered could never be my home. I was on my own from a young age. I had to work to stay alive. I almost did not stay alive. But work, and sushi, found me."

Jiro closed his eyes, gestured with a hand, "You work to find yourself, you don't find yourself in work."

He trailed off. I waited, exhibiting a degree of patience that was so unlike me.

And then he began to snore. Before I could rouse him, he shook awake.

"Mackerel should be consumed raw, and while it is absolutely fresh. Oh, we must eat soon. We must sober up. Garrett purchased horse mackerel, that's oh dear, I am feeling the room, it is *spinning*." Extra emphasis placed on the word "spinning." Garrett purchased this for us tonight. He is beginning to believe our production."

Beginning to believe our production.

A pause, and then another thought: "Mackerel's freshness is to a fault. People in this world, they want all the good in something but none of the bad. Especially in this country, people want the fresh without the fraught periods in a relationship. They think it is beauty that they want but what of the ugly? Since when has it ever been one or the other? You see someone engage in interest with something, or someone, only to undo, step away, and grow apart long before they could have cultivated anything. I once knew someone I called a friend. I suspected he had motives, yet I was lonely and in need of someone to speak to during the long nights in the park waiting for sunrise, waiting out the possibility of being mugged by one of the other homeless people navigating the park, and soon he became what I needed. I got comfortable, expecting he'd always be there to listen, be there to persuade me out of killing myself. Yet he grew tired of hearing the same thing, he would find himself too busy to return to where we survived our nights. He became too busy to look for food together, too busy to even talk…"

He started snoring again.

The camera was recording the entire time. A snore so loud it pulled him back to consciousness, back to the current thought-in-progress without skipping a beat: "People walk in and out of your life, dictated by their needs and wants for the beauty, the good and convenient, less the hard times, the care that something needs if you want it to continue to be in your life."

Jiro wiped the tears away from his eyes, opened them and looked in my direction, then back at the ceiling above, "But even though it spoils quickly and must be treated with such unrivaled care, mackerel is often the more prized of items on a sushi menu. People want more. They want what they cannot have for long. It is as if they understand the mortality of its beauty, and the beauty of being so temporary, is alluring. It is why the moment I find no interest in others I draw others in. They come to me when I have decided I want nothing to do with them. I am only alone when I need others. I am never alone when they have reason to be with me."

He shot up suddenly and dropped down from the counter, picked up the knife and began washing it. Satisfied with its cleanliness, he retrieved the mackerel.

Jiro exclaimed, "We should eat! Mackerel is very rich in vitamin-e and omega-3 oils."

Whatever you say, Jiro... We ate the sushi and then drank some more, but Jiro wasn't as talkative after the meal. To dull the punctuated silence, I played some music, mostly *Godspeed You Black Emperor,* something to drown out all my doubt. But I wasn't going anywhere.

A friend doesn't let another friend endure it alone.

One night, returning to Benihana as usual, we arrived to find out that Garrett had forgotten to leave the doors unlocked. We were stuck without any means of filming, and after standing around out back for nearly a half hour, tempting the possibility of breaking in, Jiro started talking about what waited for us in the kitchen, how it might be better that we're locked out, because "I was going to require aid from you this evening."

"Oh," I said, "what did I do now?"

My default reaction, as predicted: I did something wrong. Maybe Jiro knows. Oh shit, what could it be, things were going so well...

"Not what you did, but rather what you needed to do," said Jiro. He took a turned away from the back door and began walking the way we arrived. What else was I going to do? I followed his lead. "But rather what you would have to do to prepare tako, octopus, properly." Then he whispered into my ear.

I gasped, "No fucking way."

Jiro grinned, "Three hours of massaging the octopus. It is essential or else it's chewy and has no flavor."

"So what were you going to do while I got a workout?"

Jiro stopped short of the sidewalk and remained in the alley, "I had given some thought about taking up smoking."

"But you can't smoke in the kitchen. Wait—did you just roll your eyes at me?"

"It was a joke," said Jiro. "Come on."

"What's up?" We walked in step, or rather I matched his. Just ahead I could spot the dull green glow of the 57th F train subway station. As we approached, I slowed down, expecting to take the train like we had so many times before, but Jiro kept on, "There's nothing for us to do here tonight, so let us find something to do."

A man of complete routine, it was curious to find him in such a mood. We walked towards Central Park. "Is everything okay, Jiro?"

"Yes," he peered at the crowd on the opposite side of the street, waiting for the light to turn so that we could all do that claustrophobic near collision that always happens in midtown. There's just too many people and we all have our own momentum, walking without any real consideration of the people around us. I say this like I am any better. Consolation prize (but hold the prize): I tend to walk fast enough that I'm the one doing all the dodging.

We reached the outskirts of the park, "I will show you where I lived."

Jiro bent down near one bench, running a hand over its marred surface. "Ah! This is the one," he said, pointing to a carving of a knife, one that he presumably did, the date "10/9" next to it.

I had to ask, "What does the number stand for?"

"The date I arrived here, in America."

Jiro sat down. I prepped the camera, but then saw him shake his head slowly, "Not tonight."

"Well, alright," I nodded.

"I slept on this bench four times a week. I would go here first, because the streetlights here illuminated everything. I would not be attacked in the shadows, and the bench," he tapped one the well-worn wood, "it was near enough to the streets that no one with any street savvy would attack or be attacked this close to so many would-be witnesses. But a lot of people had the same idea. The authorities would wake me with a single strike of a baton against my shoulder. Never an arrest—too much paperwork—but they just wanted you to be invisible, to not exist, to stay in the shadows, away from the upstanding citizens."

Jiro lived in the park for five months, alternating between nine different spots (including this one). One of them was near the Woll-mann Rink, another was so deep in the park you needed to have photographic memory (or just be lucky). It was where Jiro looked to disappear, though he was sure that it was impossible because "the moment you are exhausted, this world takes from you what little you have left as tax for the sleep to follow."

The worst of it was getting mugged and beaten up. "A concussion is possible, though I was so famished and stretched thin, I could not have known the difference between lost time and merely lethargy from a lack of sustenance."

The zoo was obviously closed but Jiro said, "I would visit to commune with those that were also caught in cages. I related more to the misery of those poor animals than most hustlers and the homeless seeking escape through drugs or alcohol."

Jiro's level of passion and commitment buckled against depression and loss. "My meals were spread across two, maybe three days. I would eat something heavy, something that would make me sick. It would neutralize my hunger and taste for something appetizing. I nullified appetite so that I could not eat, even if I wanted to. The rest of the time I would smoke cigarettes and drink. I made money helping swindle food trucks. They would be so sure I was destitute and useless, they would let me attempt to turn away business from the other carts, on payment of sometimes a fairly substantial lump sum."

Jiro brought me to a secluded segment of land not too far away from the carousel. He pointed to a patch of grass, "Can you tell the difference?"

Jiro sat down, cross legged, and said, "I buried here first my booze, then my booze and anything I could not take. Then when all the booze was gone, I buried here my memories, that which I had no desire to take with me."

He dug his fingers into the soil, then looked up at me, "If you aren't going to massage octopus for hours, at least help me dig a deep hole."

It didn't take us any longer than ten minutes to dig up a tin box, rusted through. Jiro placed it in his lap and closed his eyes, "You're so curious about my past. Well," opening the tin box, "I brought it with me." In the box were a few notebooks, pictures, a wallet, and other personal items.

He made two piles—in the first, "Everything that haunts me." In the second, "The reason for every haunting." The latter consisted of little more than two notebooks, and was what received most of Jiro's attention.

He handed me the notebooks.

"You're... okay with me, umm...?"

Jiro with a single nod and then, "That is the culmination of thirty years of work. Every idea, every word—this is the progress of my work as a chef."

He raised up a picture, one of a young man wearing a suit, "See the resemblance? I lost it all to this person, my own blood."

My hands were shaking. "You know it's not too late."

"The biggest challenge," Jiro said, "is not that I cannot but more so that by the time I could, the last breaths of life will have already been taken from me. It is an envy of mine, your youth."

Shocked, I scratched at the stubble on my face, "Me?"

"Yes," he grinned, "it is good. Don't think it is a bad thing. You have so much time left. Barring illness, or tragedy, or suicide, you have so many years left to invest and discover."

I reminded him of the documentary, I reminded him of his reputation. I reminded him of all that we've already done, the filming, and the very thing so few can do: "Be genuine even after all has been gutted from you."

Jiro agreed, "You may be right."

Then I remembered the notebooks.

I opened to a random page. Written entirely in Japanese, I turned to the next page, examining the faded ink, the paper a dark brown. Perhaps Jiro was aware that it wouldn't have mattered that I glimpsed his work. Closing the notebook, I placed it down with the rest and said, "Writing down your discoveries is one thing; practicing them is another… but to put both into action, for all to see…" I shrugged, "There's really no point in slowing down now."

I picked up the camera and started recording.

This was how I met Jiro, not in the streets or in a restaurant. I met Jiro in the words we shared, the dream of there always being another chance, if you still care. I helped him discover, in fact, it was never too late to believe in immortality.

YOU WILL BUY IT FROM US, WHOLESALE

*T*here's one thing I just can't stand. Fish eggs."

"Ikura."

"Fucking fish eggs."

Jiro corrected me, "Ikura. What you speak of is a delicacy, with extra care and preservation, the flavor is unrivaled."

"Little beads that pop in your mouth."

"Have you tasted?"

We were on our way to a fish market here in Manhattan, one of the highest rated in the city (and I did my research). Jiro had told me all about the far superior offerings back in Tokyo, the Tsukiji fish market, and countless unfair comparisons between the two.

"The flavor, it is like raw egg over rice."

Give him truth and he would unearth every possible flaw. The world is a lie, just like this fish market and all its affectations claiming to be authentic. Wandering the narrow aisles of the fish market, I was amazed at the ease with which Jiro could dodge all the people here.

"Because salmon only reproduce in the fall, much of the ikura we shall be so privileged to find is frozen, preserved in soy, to retain flavor. It actually has a very smooth texture."

It was crowded, more so than even Times Square on a holiday. Or maybe it just seemed that way. So overwhelming, I couldn't concentrate on what Jiro was telling me. It was all a blur. Only when it came time for one of us to pay for something did I become a factor in the actual conversation. I had something like $400 to spend, money from selling off the books and records, my entire collection. I hoped that it was a lot but as we bought and bought and bought, stretching the sum became something of a problem, my own to figure out.

This was his moment. We couldn't skimp out on the ingredients.

Surely there was a list, though Jiro never pulled out his phone, or a piece of paper, during the entire time we wandered the market. He was directed by the same sensations that pushed me away. Like a sixth sense, he found the vendors with the best offerings, freshest possibilities. Jiro fought for a chance to speak up. This was how it always was for him, and the sooner you saw him in action the more you understood the fire within.

"The strong fish flavor may be what detracts you so much, though the use of sake to marinate separates and smooths out the strength of the taste. Though I have never chosen to dress up the ikura, I have heard of many that use cucumber slices or a quail egg to neutralize the roe's overpowering taste."

Jiro pointed to a vendor peddling what looked to be tuna. The fish had been halved and I watched as the vendor wiped either ends of the fish, wondering if this was to keep from bacteria forming or to wipe away the effects of the meat sweating. That didn't sound very appetizing and I cringed at the thought of bad meat.

"How often does one end up purchasing fish that goes bad?"

Jiro was resolute, evading three men with a slackening pace, "It is about trust. You must be able to look the vendor in the eye and see that they have the same care with their work as you do your own. I only buy from those that sell not only fish but their mission, their ideals."

We passed another vendor gutting various fish.

"Wasabi," Jiro said, out of the blue.

"Huh?"

"Wasabi."

"What's on me?"

The noise was deafening—a person to my left shouted something in a different language, causing me to jump; vendors from all sides used and abused their voices to hock their wares, as though we couldn't already see them, couldn't already smell the fish, couldn't already read the garish placement of the various signage advertising their prices.

Jiro said something else, pointed to a vendor with huge glass enclosures where live octopus swam around, many of them huddled in the far corners, frightened, tempting an escape.

"Sushi was sold on the streets, in stands, and it was made to be eaten quickly."

"Huh?" A group of five pushed me aside, maybe on purpose, and I nearly fell into one of the vendor stands. I apologized, unaware that I was already being roped into a sale.

"Sushi was popular from the start. It wasn't long before it showed up here in this city and people from all over began to understand the possibilities for flavor to be found in its pristine packaging."

Out the corner of my eye, through a partially opened warehouse door, I glimpsed whole lines of uncut, completely full fish. I moved in closer, distantly aware of a) losing Jiro in the crowd and b) perhaps this was not something I was supposed to see.

Sure enough, it was what I thought. People shouted, the discernable intensity was palpable. The noise drowned a person in waves, shaking my entire body. I watched as someone in blue roused the rest to reply with a guttural growl. I winced, thinking of the man's throat. That would hurt come tomorrow morning. Every once in a while, someone would move in, raising their hand, while most stood their ground. A few stepped aside. Four stood side by side staring intensely at the man in blue, hands raised, and then re-raised, until only one kept his hand in the air, stood prevailing over the purchase.

"They love this," Jiro appeared at my side.

Startled, I nodded, "It's fascinating."

"They like this almost more than sushi. Many strive for the cheapest price. Others for the biggest fish. Though you will find a few that seek only the finest, and often leave these bidding floors empty-handed."

Jiro pointed with his chin to an elderly looking man leaving the floor, scars on his face, the disappointment clearly hanging over every step.

"How do they survive?"

Jiro shrugged, "How does anyone?"

We couldn't stand there for too long before being noticed and escorted away from the floor. The fish market was for consumers; the bidding floor was for those looking to buy a piece of happiness. The consumers bought what the vendors deemed worth the price. Anything else is us on stage, playing our parts. Where did I fit in? This was Jiro's second home. He breezed by the vendors with a degree of zeal that could only be found in someone that understood every single ingredient from the inside out. He didn't need to hear the big sell, the vendor's peddling a story; he walked up and made a demand. If the vendor wanted his (my) money, they would have to meet that demand.

Nine times out of ten it was a no and we continued in dizzying fashion across the fish market. Yeah, I never got used to it. It was not a pleasant experience. But I was there for Jiro. I was there because it was about time I did something good for him. It was not yet time to break his heart and so I did my best to buoy it, letting it beam like it should.

The market was overwhelming in its smells, sensations, and suffocating crowds. I remember shouting at Jiro, who was maybe five people ahead of me, "We're not going to make it out of this alive!" It was probably good that he didn't hear me. Funny how the very thing he loved and enjoyed made me panic and lose all sense of calm. I wondered if it had something to do with clearly being there with Jiro, not the other way around. Ashamed maybe, of how I was ashamed of being the one trailing after Jiro throughout the market. It looked bad to no one but myself, which augmented the feeling of being erased, an afterthought in this moment, Jiro's moment.

A vendor did, and gave me a look, then tried to get me to buy shrimp.

Up ahead, Jiro had stopped at something that caught his eye. Whatever it was, I couldn't tell, it had been packaged and the vendor was ready to be paid.

Jiro turned to me, and, eyes beaming, said, "I have all I need."

This was often how our friendship worked. Jiro pointed to the shadows and I stumbled after him, using what light I could catch from his flashlight to guide me. I never had one of my own light source. For that to work, I would first have to know how to draw from the light.

Turns out what he had bought was sea urchin. Just my luck. Like the salmon roe, it was another sushi item I avoided. We left the market exhausted and carrying eight bags of various ingredients. Correction: *I* left the market exhausted. Jiro, on the other hand, talked up the storm.

"Let's walk this off," he said, arms raised as if to embrace the air around him. "I must conceive of the menu."

"You don't have it done yet?"

He snapped his fingers, "How am I to predict the offerings of the fish market? Much like every day begins new, and should never elapse in similar fashion, so too does the best markets. The catches of the day are forever different. Few understand the rhythm of the seas."

We walked down seventh avenue, nowhere in particular. I carried most of the fish, worrying slightly if they would go bad. Though they had been placed in Styrofoam coolers, you still couldn't tell. And yet, Jiro was fine with taking the chance.

Well okay.

I mentioned what happened with that one vendor that tried to sell me shrimp. I left out the humiliating part. I'm good at that: leaving out the humanity, making me look well-healed, an individual of some worth.

Jiro seemed to get a kick out of it, so I ramped up the drama a bit, "Shrimp, fresh catch, good price, buy big buy well," to a vendor forcing my hand into the tank with the live shrimp and saying, "Few understand shrimp. They are not harmless. See how much they can hurt."

Jiro laughed, "Poor sales technique." He slapped me across the right shoulder, "But shrimp is indeed misunderstood. Many believe we have an abundance of shrimp when in fact it is becoming more difficult to procure shrimp. Restaurants often devalue shrimp, making it one of the mid to lesser grade entrees, something affordable. Soon, very soon, I would not at all be surprised to discover shrimp going the way of so many others—back into the depths and shadows."

I made a point to walk in step with Jiro, unwavering even if a person in passing did not make room. I walked right into a handful of people, mostly couples holding hands, their love somehow a declaration of entitlement to be in the way of other peoples' lives.

Yeah, I was in fact upset about the experience at the fish market.

So pitiful. I cannot be happy for a friend. I must personalize something, tainting the memory with my own neuroses.

People really don't want to move out of the way.

In my way. Never in Jiro's way.

I was completely mystified how he could effortlessly walk without any need to walk around anyone. People got out of the way. They got out of the way without even realizing they were getting out of the way. Meanwhile I exhausted myself standing my ground to his left, walking in step, sure, but often having to continue and tempt a collision with strangers that took one look at me and thought, *Oh, hell no.*

"Shrimp is delicious when heated, hence is the nature of frying the fish, you would know this as tempura, and using it as a topping on sushi. I prefer not to destroy the freshness in favor of the crunchiness of it being fried. Contrary to what a lot of people think, shrimp can be eaten raw, though I prefer to have it boiled the moment before serving for maximum freshness. I am fond of any means of preparation, and it's exciting to have a sushi topping that is so resilient."

I had to project my worry onto something else, "Hey, aren't you worried we won't get to the apartment in time?"

Jiro looked at the plastic bags, "They are set with ice, it should be fine."

If that wasn't enough, I had another: "Are you sure my apartment will be good enough? I bought all the utensils and plates and pans and stuff that you texted me, but the counter is so small, and I don't think Garrett and the others will like it. How can you serve sushi in less than optimum conditions? I'm really nervous that it will ruin the scene. In fact, I insist that we do this at the restaurant. I bet Garrett will be okay with it, especially once he sees the state of my apartment. I should take a photo and send it to him. What's his phone number? I should really take a photo of just how it's such a sad kitchen. I'm already embarrassed about your reaction. You are either going to laugh or you're going to be insulted. I don't know which. I think you'll laugh and then be insulted. Nobody laughs after being insulted. That doesn't make any sense. They gag or feel nauseous. They don't laugh. I should really call Garrett. Can you give me his number?"

Commence panic attack in five, four, three, two...

I paused right in the middle of the sidewalk. I coughed and fumbled around in my pockets looking for my phone. When I couldn't find it, terror bubbled to the surface.

Tears formed on my face.

I started apologizing, "I'm sorry, I'm so sorry..."

One of the bags brushed up against the pant-legs of a person passing by. I recall this image more than most because of the thought that joined it—people might step on the fish. It launched me into another panicked display: someone creating a blockade with their body, as if the bags were a dead body, and I was attempting to clear the scene.

I kept repeating, "I'm sorry, I'm so sorry..."

I made eye contact with random strangers.

"I'm sorry, I'm so sorry..."

Imagine how bad I looked. One of those moments where you wished you could be put out of your own misery. If something were to be erased, please make it this moment. Instead I'm writing about it, wishing it were fiction.

35 years old and nothing to show for it. All my friends married with children or married to their careers, married to their success— insert all the usual suspects.

But I don't have any friends so this doesn't involve me.

Wow, that's so depressing to think about.

I just needed my phone. I needed to know how to prevent all of this from happening, and breaking everything we've worked so hard to create. My confession, it would potentially destroy everything. It was all over. This was it. The moment I come clean.

Panic in full, I screamed out every word, feeling it in my throat.

Where was Jiro during all of this?

He was across the street, watching from afar, filming it using my phone. He hadn't heard my confession. Jiro was busy creating the menu, he talked highly of shrimp, of the sea urchin, of the fatty tuna he would prepare to his liking, which was "controversial because you never deviate from tradition. I can do nothing but deviate from tradition. Tradition led me here, innovation will be the one to point the way forward. I will no longer be led astray."

My confession erased, and yet—while I should have been relieved, it made things more difficult, forever on the tip of my tongue, readying to slip out between sentences.

How much longer could I take this?

GOOD INTENTIONS

*T*hankfully we didn't use my kitchen. Jiro had told me Garrett preferred that we have the ideal, which I assumed was the Benihana kitchen. We were given the keys to a sushi establishment in Greenwich Village, the owner being a friend of Garrett's. The place would be closed between the hours of 2 and 6PM and so it was slotted to be our moment to film. The preparations would last the entire day, into the night. Everything prepped at Benihana and we'd Uber as quickly as possible to the Village. I could see just how disconcerting this was for Jiro's standards of freshness and ideal preparation but instead of stress, Jiro was absolute, "It is only a failure if we are unable to adapt."

We remained silent most of the ride. I spotted the driver looking back at us via the rearview mirror. Avert your gaze, eye contact kept at a minimum. I remembered my role in this. As director, I should be the one helping, not looking for a helping hand.

Since the fish market, since that moment in the street, I had become so subdued.

Jiro had noticed, though wouldn't say much about it, instead focusing on the gargantuan task ahead. It was the sort of thing that used to rouse me.

Nourished by his enthusiasm, I no longer had the energy coursing through my veins. The end should have come later, and yet I could feel it ending with every incoming breath. The good times were coming to an end, and I didn't want to admit it yet.

Something. Say something.

I offered some encouragement, motivation if you will—

"Tonight, let's push it all aside. This is *your restaurant*. This is your craft and you've spent a life laboring over it. The latter is truth, but tonight there's no place for trivialities."

Way to go. That's the best you can do?

Jiro gave me a nod and returned to his thoughts. I could see it rolling across his face. So much was happening. In between us were the coolers, the compartments carrying the marinades, the fish, the rice. I lightly pressed the palm of my hand against the heated metal of the container that held the rice.

"It must be served at body temperature."

"Oh," I said.

Perhaps he knew more about me than I thought. I had said this before, but never really believed it. I'm sure most would pity me. That is, if you didn't hate me first.

"I will have to place the rice in a different container upon arrival." I could hear it in his voice. "Everyone assumes the rice must be cold. They often don't know what it takes to prepare rice, the vinegar added, the techniques necessary to maintain the perfect texture. The temperature has a lot to do with it." He talked away the tension.

A word came to mind. "Umami."

"Yes," also placing a palm against the container, "the balance of flavors is of utmost importance. It mustn't be hastened or else the act of umami will not be achieved."

The same expressionless face stared out the window, deep in thought. If it were me, I would be jittery, my voice thin and cracking, and I wouldn't be able to concentrate.

"Looks like we'll arrive in ten minutes," I said.

The driver ran a hand through his course hair, "I can get you there quicker."

Jiro dismissed this, "Ten minutes is fine."

We got there in five. I helped carry in the coolers. Garrett was already there, waiting for us in the front of the restaurant. "Hey," he waved to me, but just as quickly moved to Jiro, giving a proper greeting, complete with a hug and a conversation that lasted a couple minutes. I couldn't hear what they were talking about, Garrett keeping his voice low, which triggered bad thoughts, jealousy, and a scenario to play out in my mind where Garrett whispers my confession, the truth, to Jiro at this, the most inopportune of occasions.

"I got it," Garrett shook his head when I tried to help carry in the containers.

"You sure?"

But maybe he didn't hear me. I stood outside, attempting to stay calm. Four containers held in my hands, none of them individually that heavy, but together, coupled with how long I stood out there, became enough to send pain signals up my arms.

It was a form of self-inflicted torture. Thoughts came to mind about different types of torture methods, like water torture, water boarding, hazing techniques where frat dudes forced the newcomers to hold a bunch of stuff out in either direction, causing them to fight the impossible limits of gravity, tearing muscles and inflicting pain.

Lots of pain.

I didn't want to go inside.

You could have seen it on a sign or billboard or spelled out across the sky. By the end of this, it'll all be over. He'll get his meal, and we will film it, it's all set up. I showed up earlier this morning with the camera, lights, and made sure everything was operational.

Look at me, I had become an actual director and writer.

We've come a long way. The script is basically finished.

It has all fit together, every scene, each puzzle piece. Jiro let me use some of the notebook pages and pictures he had hidden from the world. I could see it all now:

The documentary as a finished product.

But where there should be my name, credited as director, it would be left blank.

My name would not grace a single frame of this. I would remain nameless, much like I am nameless in this entire narrative. It's what I deserve.

I could see the title, and then Jiro's face.

Dreams of Being, a dream carried from a young age, the dream became destination—a fact—and only now, late in life, a life stolen by his own flesh and blood, did he recover its source. Dreams of being something more than the days that stack up, forming a life that could be inked in like an expiration date. The epitaph and obituary must say more than name and cause of death. There must be something more to the life well-lived.

Jiro's dream carries him through his days. You dream of being something more than the stuff you take from the world, because we all take from the world a piece of it that cannot be regained. We must be selfish if we are to become a person, and in doing so, we leave a mark.

Some of us, we just dream of that mark being one that makes for a better picture.

Garrett poked his head out, "Yo, the hell you doing?"

Holding back a sigh, I say, "Be right there."

"Come on, come on!"

Well, here goes nothing…

Jiro made sure I couldn't watch him make the final preparations. I was forced to stay out with the rest, behind the camera, where I would remain. I wouldn't eat the sushi. The biggest meal, the one that we worked so hard on, the one moment to punctuate an entire series of events, and I wasn't allowed to take part. There's something poetic in that—how it was Jiro's muted way of punishing me for what I had done.

Before dining, of course, you had to play out those niceties, the introductions. "Oh, my sincerest apologies, but I cannot shake your hand." Jiro wasn't having any of it. Garrett didn't even skip a beat. "He must keep his hands the same temperature. If he shakes yours and yours, and Tashi's and Nick's, it will change the temperature of his touch."

"Damn, that's intense."

"I wasn't aware there was so much that went into making sushi."

I chimed in, "There's a whole world."

Garrett looked over, said nothing.

Jiro addressed his audience:

"I have made sushi for decades. When I wake up, the first thing I think of is sushi and the last thing I think about before sleep is sushi. I used to have so many ideas, I would consistently turn away from my current task and write them down. Sushi demanded so much of me, and I in turn demanded so much from it. My life had become the sushi I learned to make, and it was not until I had mastered what it means to make the egg sushi, and see it across my master's face, that I finally accepted my role as apprentice and a shokunin. Life for me was work. The passion came later. I would sacrifice anything to meet the increasing demands of my art and work. Until it was removed from me, and therefore I removed myself from both my work, art, and home, I had experienced a degree of success. I was able to start a restaurant of my own, and design a menu of sushi that became the most desirable for many seeking new sushi. On the surface, I made sushi that looked identical to others, if even simpler than the many. But beneath the simplicity I sought the perfection of flavors. I have not achieved it, and I may never do so, but in the years of remaining quiet, in the solitude of America, my passion has not waned. I am more passionate than ever before, and I owe it to many, but more so I must continue making sushi as a means of showing my appreciation for all that believed in me. Thank you for taking the time out of your day to dine with me."

With a bow, he turned his attention to the sushi.

It was like he was in another world, saved from ours.

He was so calm as he spoke, and even calmer as they introduced themselves. I was jealous.

Frankly, I'm still jealous.

I want to know what that feels like. More than understanding the sacrifices and needs of living the life of a shokunin, I want to know what the pay-off feels like. If Jiro were still here, still talking to me, I bet he'd point out my jealousy is the reason why I'll never get there. I will never know what it feels like to transcend and live in a world you created.

Oh yeah, and the other people here?

Garrett you already know.

Tashi invested in restaurants across Manhattan. He was quick to say the names but for virtue of just not liking the guy and the size of his ego, I'm not going to mention them here.

Nick was another investor, someone that owned a few restaurants, most of them Asian, and nearly all of them ramen joints, which in his words, "Asian food's the best. Asians are the best. Superior people. It's a fact!" Never mind how racist that sounds, and is, hearing this and seeing how all of them were basically investors just drove the point even further that I probably wouldn't be seeing as much from Jiro soon.

John, guess what, yup: Another investor. He likes to play golf, go sailing, probably likes to get laid by all kinds of random "chicks," and basically all the other clichés rich assholes like him do to flaunt their richness.

Nolan, on the other hand, caught me off guard. He was a director. When Garrett mentioned the reason for this, how we needed stand-ins, the ulterior motive was to find Jiro a backer, this wasn't a mystery to anyone there that day. This guy though, Nolan, he claimed to be intrigued by the production.

"I've done two feature films, and working hard on the third. It's not going well, but I bet you know how that is!" He said this to me offhand, after the meal.

"You know where you're doing post?"

I didn't follow.

"Production. Post production."

"Ah," I tried to laugh it off, "mind's a little spent, long day."

He wouldn't let it go, "Where at? I'm looking for a new place to edit, myself."

"I'll do a mix of it at, my place and at my friend's." Yeah, sounds believable.

"Does you or your friend have a studio?"

I pretended to be busy with the camera, checking the framing, or something.

Of course, I didn't have an answer. "Don't we all?" And then excused myself, walking outside, pretending to take a call.

Garrett gave a glowing intro for Jiro, claiming ownership of the entire idea of the documentary. He talked about how he met Jiro, and how Jiro might not be the best performer, which makes it hard working at Benihama—"seriously guys, invest in Jiro, save him from having to continue working for me!"—but his cooking is unrivaled. "Usually, when you take a chef on you need to give them a relatively extended probationary period where they don't really cook at the same rate as the rest. They should demonstrate their ability to handle the entire meal. It can be quite taxing doing teppanyaki. But Jiro, he walked in on the first day and made the best teppanyaki I have ever

tasted." He went on and on but eventually, empty stomachs and en-
lightened minds demanded Jiro do what he does best.

This was the moment where you see the lining, the ending still
somewhere over the horizon, a little ways off, but the yellow tape was
already being rolled out—the scene of the crime right there, right
fucking there. Yes, I would tell not only Jiro but everyone in the entire
world. I would tell everyone through the words Jiro wouldn't say, and
I would tell everyone in the walks I would once again find myself lost,
broken, the same, who knows.

And just like that, the first course began.

Jiro never looked happier than when he was making sushi. You can
talk so much about what good sushi is but that's all it is: talk. To me,
good sushi is the very thing that brings a smile to one's face. The meal
worked in three movements. I had no idea what to expect. In the
script, the area where the meal transpires, all I had was a card with a
doodle of dollar signs, the money shot.

The mystery was alluring to me, as it always was when I encoun-
tered a new mystery. It doesn't happen often but when it does, you
don't just let it pass you by. You look into it. Or in my case, you lie and
lead a fake life and you consider the eye of a camera and press record.

I seldom panned away from Jiro—the fuckers eating the meal
would remain faceless, by my choice. Though his face retained that
irrefutable expressionless gaze, Jiro's eyes lit up. The camera loved it.
This was the sort of thing that brought a luster to a rarity, while often
none to most. The enigma, the allure: It came from the very thing we
are all searching for.

We want to care about something.

Seeing someone care so much, it's attractive. It attracts an audience. It attracts… investors.

The meal commenced in silence. Garrett hushed Nick at one point, pressing a finger to his lips. We opted to play some music. Classical music, something I didn't recognize.

The first movement consisted of the usual items, the stuff I liked the best. For someone that likes mystery, I sure am predictable and risk-averse. But again, I have already established the fact that I'm a hypocrite and a bad person so—yeah that's how that sentence ends.

Jiro in motion was a sight to behold. The way he took each topping, swiftly reaching for just the right amount of rice, the wasabi grazed on the innermost side of the topping, to be hidden between the rice and meat, the elegance of each motion as he pressed two fingers into the shape of the sushi, then pressed on either side of the sushi, again and again, the repetition to be dealt with every piece created, it was a marvel. This masterwork was wasted on these people, and yet these people would be the ones to give a master their due. The master still needed to survive, still needed to have a foundation. You could be a Jedi master and you still needed a roof over your head. You still needed to eat. I guess what I am trying to say is that this was all so bittersweet.

First piece he makes is halibut, and he does say something to break the silence, explaining each piece with little more than the name, the true name, and what they should be tasting. He gave the camera the words to describe the flavors that otherwise would have been uncanny yet impossible to comprehend.

Halibut, hirame, a light earthy flavor, it can be chewy, but otherwise soft.

The next piece was squid.

I noticed little slits cut into each piece and remembered one of our conversations where he mentioned how difficult it is to keep hold of some fish. He explained that abalone was notably difficult to hold, same with squid. Cutting slits into each piece made it so that the tip of the finger could have something to push into. Fascinating to see what facts are remembered and how anything, something random or not, can cause them to rise to the surface of one's memory.

Horse mackerel, then finally the best, the one that made my mouth water from behind the camera: Tuna. He made each piece one at a time. I watched as each popped the sushi in their big fat mouths and ate it without any attention to just how amazing it was that they could taste perfection. After the tuna, akami, came another piece of tuna. Chu-toro, medium tuna.

I repeated the phrase, "This is not about me," in my mind throughout the meal.

My stomach growled. I hadn't eaten all day, expecting that I would be part of this course.

After the tuna came... another piece of tuna.

We have now reached peak jealousy.

O-toro, or fatty tuna, is frequently the most popular sushi. If you go to any sushi restaurant and get a spicy tuna roll or something with tuna in it, odds are you are getting cuts of fatty tuna. When you think of sushi, you think of fatty tuna. There's just no other way around it.

Gizzard shad, or Kohada. By now, the groove of the meal had been set and the establishing shot had long since been abandoned for closer views of the sushi itself. There's a reason why Instagram is full of food photos. People love porn and that includes the variety where you stare at pictures of other people's food and wish you were eating that very thing.

I was there as a voyeur, there to capture every delicacy.

By the time the second movement elapsed, I was faint, low blood sugar, obvious that I needed something to eat. There is a metaphor in this, I'm sure of it.

The second movement consisted of fresh catches of the day which meant hamaguri, or clam, and shima-aji, or striped mackerel. The only thing I couldn't capture on film was the actual taste of the sushi. I did not have the ability to capture the smells of the sushi. Every single piece had its own presence. Every piece designed by hand to induce the heights of all five senses.

Some fish was served raw, others cooked. Jiro did all of this himself, which caused this meal to be so unique. Where apprentices usually helped with preparation, there was only Jiro.

"The second movement," Jiro said, "is one where I am able to improvise. I fill the center of the meal with new ideas, newly informed flavors."

This meant kurma ebi, or wheel shrimp. Damn, I could go for some shrimp right now. I still remember watching as Jiro stuffed the rice into the shrimp and that brush of soy sauce vaulting across it, a single brushstroke to introduce the union of a new pairing.

Next, he made sayori, or half-beak, and then tako, octopus, which again triggered a memory from recent past. Jiro appointing me as his apprentice that one night, where my duty was to massage for multiple hours until it became tender, less chewy.

The third movement was the finale. The flavors overwhelmed the taste buds and Jiro offered that they eat a little ginger to clean the palate. John asked for alcohol, which received a frown from Garrett and then an explanation from Jiro about how drinking powerful drinks like beer or a whiskey ruins the flavors of the sushi.

"That's some bullshit," John stammered, "Every single restaurant serves alcohol, and that includes sushi joints too."

Jiro remained calm and vigilant, explaining it again, this time slower, and more precise, as if to let John in on a secret.

He calmed down the moment Jiro placed the saba, or mackerel, on John's plate. You can keep talking or you can take this piece of sushi and put it in your mouth. You bet it shut them up. It silenced all disdain. Food has a way of enlightening the soul. After the mackerel came the uni, or sea urchin. Even with the hunger I cringed when I saw the bright yellow.

After the urchin came bay scallops, or ko bash ra. This proved to be a real hit for Tashi, who exhaled audibly, a gesture of umami.

The salmon roe caused Nick to hesitate, "No, I think I'll pass on this one."

Jiro's reaction, "It is deemed a sign of disrespect to deny what the itamae offered you."

John said, "If he doesn't want it, I'll eat it."

I muttered to myself, *Just eat the fucking sushi.*

Garrett said the same thing, but actually, you know, said it, "Just eat the fucking sushi!"

Apologies followed by Nick taking the sushi, gagging at first, but then realizing it wasn't as bad as expected.

The final three pieces are anago, or salt-water eel, kanpyo-maki, dried gourd roll, and the egg sushi, which is called tamagoyaki. By the end of the meal, everyone asked for more. Much to my surprise, they didn't ask for more tuna. Most requested was mackerel and salmon roe, though I think the latter was requested by one of the others to mess with Nick. There was a brief exchange of glances, all in Nick's direction, followed by hushed laughter.

At the end of the meal, Jiro did not bow. It was deafeningly silent. There was no indication that the meal had concluded until Jiro took a step back from the counter.

Everyone clapped. They continued clapping long after what was customary.

Jiro looked in John's direction, "*Now* is the time for sake."

By all accounts the meal was a success. Discussion continued, drinks were poured. Garrett excused himself and left the room.

Jiro turned to the camera and asked, "Oh, you're still filming?"

If the camera was rolling, I still had a purpose. I belonged here, even if only in the background. A person can get themselves to believe anything. I had achieved a special level of deceit—I had taken all that was false and made it fact for everyone that was a part of it. I could tell from the faintness in my voice when I agreed to follow Jiro into the kitchen, and in each shaky step, I was not long for this scene. This is where my part would end. But we had to share one last heartfelt moment, just to make this that much harder to do.

Jiro burst into tears.

"Jiro..."

"I had forgotten," he whimpered, "this is the best night of my life."

"It's a lot," I said.

"I feel so overwhelmed."

All I could muster up was a few short replies, "Yeah," and "It's a lot." Some help I was.

You hold out on joy in the same way you balance a check book; though you pay the bills and spend some on leisure, you always save face, keeping one foot in and one foot out, something for a rainy day. Jiro had lived destitute and near the downward spiral for so long it became all that he knew. Keep on the same sequence of repression and complaint and it becomes you. To see him break down like this was not surprising. Overwhelming, yes, but what became a surprise was how he hugged me, didn't need to tell me anything because he seemed to think I would already know.

It made me cry too.

I cried for an entirely different reason.

"I don't know what to do," he said.

"Oh, that part is simple: You go back out there and you listen to them sing your praises."

But that wasn't it, he meant about what was ahead for him, "I cannot keep doing this. I cannot be invisible anymore."

"And you won't be," I promised, "good things are ahead."

Jiro laid down on the kitchen counter.

"It's okay to take some time," I said, standing there, unable to move, not sure what to do.

I could hear them all in the other room, chatting and laughing, and soon Jiro would join them, carrying the news that I was to remain in the kitchen, unseen. I was to remain in the kitchen never again to be allowed in their lives.

"It was a success. You were a success. The documentary will be a success."

What I really meant was: "I'm about to hurt you. I'm about to push you over the edge. I'm about to be the reason why you might never want to trust another person ever again."

I wandered around the kitchen. What else could be said. Why did I want to tell him now, anyway? Think about this for a second. Kick him when he's already vulnerable, break apart a moment that should have been breathtaking.

Jiro's arm was draped across his face, shielding his eyes from the fluorescent light above. That's when it hit me. I wanted to tell him now because I was no longer in the spotlight. The whole production, and his mission, his dream, it had outplayed my role. Maybe I was always second to Jiro, but at least I had played the role of his co-star. So much had changed.

The real star was the sushi, and who else but Jiro could do anything about that?

"I destroyed mine and look how well I'm doing?"

Jiro sounded tired, "I was able to prepare and deliver an entire omakase menu all by myself. I couldn't manage to do that even when I was younger, much younger."

I could have said anything.

Jiro sat back up, "I am beginning to have ideas again!"

"Being nothing," I spoke louder, "has its benefits."

"The ideas used to be so prevalent, but they disappeared the moment I stopped preparing sushi that would be served to customers, to those that hadn't tasted my trials and errors."

"With nothing, you can once again become everything. It's no longer a lie if you have nothing to line it up with, no story of your past, no biography at all to call on by name."

"It has been so long," Jiro wiped away the tears, "since I have been able to consider a customer. I haven't looked anyone in the eye in twenty years."

112

I pointed the camera at Jiro, mostly to get his attention. "The beauty of having no name is that when you are caught on camera, nobody can see you. They cannot see you for who you really are. All they see is a nameless person, a cameo, an uncredited role."

Jiro looked at me, drew in deeply, exhaled, "I needed this. I really needed this. I had forgotten how much of my soul is in the sushi I make. Maybe if life were twice as long, I might have done things differently."

Into the camera now, a close shot of one of my eyes. I offered him a fantasy, "You could say anything you want because it's not in the script. No one is going to question the odd actions of an individual whose existence is to ruin those of all they encounter." A pause, and then: "Perhaps in another universe, you are a celebrated and award-winning chef and the documentary is not one of desperation but a design of merit."

Jiro sighed, "Perhaps there's still time."

"Perhaps in another universe I have a name and I am not in fact about to lose the only thing in life giving me meaning. Perhaps in another universe I am interviewing you and we are getting to know each other by our art." I looked up from the camera, to a Jiro looking at me intently.

"It's okay," he said. "Go ahead and say it."

I mumbled, "Another universe would be so lucky."

We had only an hour left before having to clear out for the commencement of the restaurant's hours of operation. Turns out finally telling the truth can be done in five minutes or less. I said every single word. Bookended by "I'm sorry," it comes out in a blaze, like setting fire to this book and believe me I have tempted it more than once. The only way to be sure was to turn the camera on myself, the confession in full.

I talked about how I had never directed before. I talked about my failure as a writer. I talked about everything I could think of where I created instead of giving truth the command.

After it was over, I looked away from the camera and saw that Jiro had left the kitchen. I listened for his voice among those in the other room. I listened for a long time, trying to find the strength to make my next move. I listened for something, anything to point me in the right direction. I looked at a bottle of whiskey on the shelf. I reached for it. Hungry, it would give me courage. Hungry, a few gulps would get me completely drunk. I was about to attend a funeral. Where there should be a body there is instead the idea of our friendship.

You see I had something in my hands. If I couldn't do it myself I would let the camera do all the talking. Like the press of every key to get this down before it's gone, I was *still* filming.

I missed my friend.

I missed all that we had done.

Holding back tears, I watched from behind the camera, from behind the sushi bar, from behind the scenes the unraveling of our friendship. I saw it before everyone else, much like it was sinful to carry on knowing of a future demise long since been predicted.

I missed the days where I would pay for Jiro's meals and he would slam the entire establishment, finding fault in all that they featured. I missed the days when we wouldn't talk at all and I thought not about the lie but the project as something real. I missed the moments he shared with me, showing his own broken past.

I missed Jiro the same way a person finally recognizes which moments were the best in their life. You never see it until its long gone, and in its stead, you have only that emptiness. You have only the memories, and sooner than you think, those leave you too.

I missed this moment, the one that just passed.

RUNAWAY: A NOVEL

T hen the mind starts racing and because it does, my body does
the same. I started running away from the kitchen and away from
the restaurant, and away from the life the last couple months.

I ran a familiar route, one I used to walk, the same one that Jiro
and I had navigated not too long ago. Benihana wasn't too far away
from here. I ran in the opposite direction, heading uptown, into Har-
lem, and pushed myself to the limit. I played out a variety of scenari-
os, all of them leading the same conclusion where I am deemed unfit
to be around people, specifically those I care about.

Version one went like this:

Jiro walked out of the kitchen after he heard one line of my confession and simply wanted nothing to do with it. By not believing
it, he carried the lie, preferring it to any truth. That would mean my
running away would cause a disturbance. Maybe he looked for me,
called and texted me, but my phone remained silent. No new messages, no new voicemail.

Version two was far more deliberate:

Jiro heard the confession and immediately went to the others,
specifically Garrett, and in hearing the truth they all returned to the

kitchen, only to find me missing. They stand around and for a second all wonder if they had imagined me. If I wasn't a real person. Jiro, who should know better, takes a second to think about it. Just like that—erased.

Version three involved the camera:

They return to the kitchen, furious, only to find the camera, which I in fact had left, and they press play. They play back the footage and where there should be a rousing of anger and discussion of possible legal action, there is instead just silence and the sound of my voice. And then the image of Jiro slowly but surely falling to the ground, defeated.

Version four involved Jiro:

He listened and understood and maybe always did, my lies being as I predicted: his too. He left the kitchen because it wasn't anything new to procure from the telling. I was no longer of any worth to him. He had investors to appease, and the idea, the obsession, the lone item of worth in his life. He had lied too, and in this version, he lied because it was more convenient than having to tell me things weren't going to get any better. No, things would remain the same (for me).

Version five was about me:

In it, they all stand around watching the confession.

Minutes go by before someone, I figure John, chimes in, "Who is this?"

More time passes and then Garrett says, "Is this going anywhere?"

And that is the real concern. That was always the real concern. My life, and the things I created, never going anywhere. Why become a storyteller, a writer, if you have no interest to expose and empathize?

More silence, more time passing, and where Jiro is supposed to be heartbroken, he is instead, numb, no reaction at all.

He answers John's question, "A sad person."

Garrett dismisses the entire thing and leaves the room. It is as though I am not someone they recognize. It plays out like this in my mind, frame for frame, and it could all become reality. In fact, I might as well take it at face-value, what really happened.

I am a fraud.

Jiro is a genius.

It takes more than being a genius to be a success. It requires tenacity, authenticity, and sacrifice. The makings of a genius are born along with the being themselves, but it takes a dream to make it whole.

As I ran, I stripped away every lie. There went the possibility of a directorial debut. Turning the corner, I tossed aside the thought of this work being the one that dug both Jiro and I out of ou r rut. Running a red light, go ahead hit me, I dare you, I dropped the feeling that I wasn't alone in this city. Like so many other runners, I was the image of a lone body, arms pumping, legs pulling along the mind. You never saw people running with hands held, with a mind to share with others.

When a person runs, they run alone.

Out of breath, my lungs burning, I erased every aspect of the routine we had employed, all those drunken nights, the stories shared, the philosophies born. And then finally, I removed myself from the documentary.

I thought I heard someone call out my name. Turning to look, I tripped, my shoulder breaking the fall. The collision jogged free a memory from early on, when Jiro still doubted me. We sat facing the same direction, waiting for our ramen to arrive.

He asked me for my name but I changed the subject. Later, after he told me a bit about his past, he asked for me to do the same. I managed to direct the conversation to the ramen we had just finished eating.

I caught my breath, thinking about how I never told Jiro a single thing about myself.

My body aching, I returned to a pace I was most familiar with. I walked until I reached the water. I could do it, right here—jump and drown. It would take effort though.

Leave out the trial, just keep the error.

It couldn't have been healthy, that I erased every memory, every word of encouragement he tirelessly imparted. The many hours texting each other, and just as many in person where he spoke to me about finding the spirit in the source, teaching me by revealing his own tragedies.

We had been through a lot.

All the while, I was too busy indulging in the great big lie to enjoy the moment, to listen and employ his advice. What was he trying to tell me, all this time? He tried to tell me not to live in fear. He tried to tell me to be myself, no matter how vulnerable.

He tried to tell me that it's not too late, it's never too late.

It wasn't what I wanted to hear.

Yes, I thought this would lead somewhere. Unlike all my walks, it would lead to being in someone's life, a part of rather than merely orbiting it.

Misery loves company, but even I couldn't seem to keep anyone around.

No matter the version, I am replaced, the documentary continuing unabated. I am replaced and Jiro is not.

Like a breaking news story, I saw it stream across every surface:

Nolan takes over the documentary. Without much effort, Nolan replaces me in Jiro's memory. The documentary retains the same title, but Nolan's name sits side by side Jiro's. John and Tashi invest in a restaurant where Jiro can explore the limits of what sushi and his mind can manufacture. Nick sells the rights for all sorts of merchandise and cookbooks. The empire Jiro deserved, finally a destination forged by redemption.

I am exactly what I joked so much about, a ghost. Don't cut yourself in the process. Once you break the skin, you never stop bleeding.

Believe me or don't, but in this case, I am *actually* telling the truth.

It may be the one time I do, and it's in the pages of a book no one will ever read.

CITY AS MAXIMUM FIELD

*T*hings go well for others, especially people you know. You want to be happy for them. To some degree you are. But eventually there are no more phone calls, text messages. No more communication from the one person you might have called friend.

The person you care about most, more than your own self, won't talk to you. Doesn't want anything to do with you, and no—it's not their fault.

It's yours. It has always been you that builds these boundaries, forges this distance.

Loneliness won't hide you from those haunting thoughts. The nightmares amass best when there's nothing to distract you. The haunting thoughts become all you have.

This is all to say that I was back to wandering the city. I walked the same long mornings and extended afternoons, taking each step quick in succession like I was meant for somewhere, when really where I stood with pause, waiting for a streetlight to change, was perhaps good enough, the best it'll ever get. I walked the city but this time, I had a purpose. I looked for Jiro in the faces of the many.

I searched everywhere.

The day after the dinner, I didn't leave bed. I stayed in, coming up with excuses for my hunger, my need to use the bathroom. I held it all in, every urge and every worry, like they would leave me too, never again to resurface. It is horrific to think such thoughts, but you can't help not to, and never realize the severity of it until you're finally outside of it. I crawled to the bathroom, believing that if I was visible in any window, something might happen, as though they were right there, watching and waiting to say it to my face. Just tell me I'm a piece of shit.

Appetite completely disappears. There's nothing left to be done so I do nothing. I fade in and out of consciousness until I am severely awake, to the point where I cannot even shut my eyes for more than an instant. The thought continued to creep up on me:

Jiro knows.

Jiro knows.

He knows now. *Everyone* knows.

After the first day, I could leave the bed but I couldn't leave my bedroom. By day three, I could enter the common area of my apartment, but I would only do so when my other roommates weren't home. The end of the first week, I could walk a couple blocks without shivering, without becoming too paranoid and turning back. The middle of week two, I could eat again, but not sushi. Not yet. And still, it would be a month before I even looked at a menu.

When you stop talking to people, it changes the way you think. Everything becomes more insular, roaming around thoughts that never need to be put into language. I would feel and let it be felt, but if someone were to ask me what, precisely, I was feeling, I wouldn't be able to give a phrase, much less a whole sentence. I had always been the sort of person that thinks in language. Most of us do. Our thoughts immediately translate into words, on the ready if you needed to speak or write them down. When thoughts don't have language to be tethered to, they become unruly. Every thought blends in with a feeling. When both feed on each other, that's how a panic attack starts.

I had the blank page and so much to say but with no language to say it.

This is how the book started.

I borrowed another person's voice. I tried finding it first in books, but I couldn't handle the confidence in other writers' voices. I tried eavesdropping conversations on the street, but I feared that they would take from me more than I could take from them. My life lingered around such a small little two-block world for a good month, maybe two. I was that person you see numerous times a day walking by but forget the moment they leave your view.

I found the voice in the audio notes I kept. I found the voice within those days of meaning, when dreams of being a writer/director were almost palpable.

I borrowed, once again, from Jiro, this time his voice. I spoke to the blank screen and, visibly sobbing, I tried calling him to no avail. It went to voicemail, but I couldn't bear to leave even a single "hello."

He had record of my call, right there, on his phone, another notification.

I wondered where he was at that particular moment. This is the part I can't tell—the part of the story from which I am banned from knowing. It is my punishment, my curse. I will never know what became of the documentary, what became of my work, the work that had become so real, so impassioned, I began to believe my own lies.

I will find out later, but only in testimonies from others that tread lightly when speaking of the topic. I will never be privy to what happened right after I ran away like a coward.

The coward remains in the dark.

That's kind of the point.

With a silent promise, I borrowed Jiro's voice and began writing down every thought. I forced myself to relearn how to write, how to speak, and I don't mean simple statements like: "I feel okay" and "I ate breakfast." I mean whole paragraphs walking around and eventually through the dark neighborhoods of my own nightmares.

One day I am remembering the first lie and then the next day, I'm remembering the night in Central Park. Then I found myself remembering Jiro's stories and memories as my own, as if I had been the one to live them. That's when it became dangerous. That was when I stopped and deleted every word and started over.

For once, be yourself.

I spent another month doing nothing but breaking down my anxieties and paranoia, which exacerbated the condition, making it feel like I was relapsing into a depression somehow even more decimating than before. Fight it, fight it, you have to fight it.

Thankfully I did, somehow. I could attribute it to the writing, and it's probably true, but there was no one there to congratulate me, just like there will be no one here when I finish this book, when I finally step away, and move on to nothing. There won't be anyone because I'm stupid enough to think, even for a second, there should have been someone at all.

Just when I'm about to feel okay, seeing forward to later that day, looking forward to the next couple hours, I remember:

Jiro knows.

Everyone knows.

The latter no longer interests me. This book I'm writing, it began out of fear, and then continued out of need. If I finish it, it won't be for catharsis or for some bigger goal. If I ever finish, it will be due to no longer having anything left to say.

This was how I learned to walk through the city of my thoughts and fears.

This was how I discovered that things do in fact heal.

Some take time. Most leave barely a scar.

Jiro knows. People will forgive you, but they don't admit to no longer wanting to have anything to do with you. Forgiveness as an escape. Forgiveness as an exit plan, a red light above a door that upon walking through cannot be opened from the opposite side.

I walked the city developing a hunger, an appetite for avoidance. I wrote whole passages of this book in my head and would recite them until it was all I could hear, the lines repeating as I circled the block, once, twice, three times, my destination already having been reached, a restaurant that could satiate the hunger, a meal I needed, having not eaten in the last day and a half. I walked the block a fourth time, only because I couldn't face what was inside. I couldn't fathom talking to anyone, not even for something as simple as a reply to the question, "May I take your order?"

I couldn't be sure I would know what to order, much less what I wanted.

I walked with these words, the aforementioned paragraph, circling in my head, until I found myself on a block in the Meatpacking District I hadn't walked before. So like, tell me this, your honest opinion: Is it strange that when I find a block, find myself where I didn't expect to be, it happened to be a block devoid of anything but liquor stores?

One after the other, if it wasn't a bar, it was a liquor store.

The world trying to tell me something.

What else did I have to do today?

I was the person standing outside the liquor store, looking through the barred storefront window, trying to fight off the urge of what I was about to do.

I had all the sentences in my head to write down. I held onto my phone, which hadn't received a notification in three days. I was the sort of person that kept track of that stuff. Like pretty much anything else, eventually your lies, your deception, your true self, comes out.

People figure you out or you fumble and reveal your entire hand, including the cards you keep solely for yourself. Keep feeling sorry for yourself but it won't change anything.

Okay, enough of that. I combated these interludes quite often. I wondered if it would get better with time. More like I had some better days but most of the time it blanketed every move. Anything could trigger such thoughts. Okay, I went into the liquor store. I stood in line. With each passing minute, I became more anxious, more worried about what it meant to be someone standing buying liquor at 10AM on a Tuesday. You will drink, and you will be merry...

It takes me approximately three shots to start seeing everything with that delightful haze. Forget eating, I would supplement myself with the liquor diet.

This is what I think about when trying to avoid what I'm really thinking about. The moment I took a drink and realized I had made it past the hundred-page mark, my first thought was, "I can still fuck this up." My second thought was, "I need a drink."

I bought cheap Evan Williams, averting my gaze from the side of the shelf where the sake was stored. Denial is one of the first stages of the grieving process. I had a long way to go.

With this bottle, I had given myself pardon from the rest of the day. I no longer wandered, instead nearly ran to the nearest subway stop, attempted to hide the black plastic bag as much as possible. Imagine people on their way to work or to a meeting seeing me for what I had become, a nervous drunk. I looked the part of one on their way out, rather than way in. And sure, I didn't really try that hard to hide it. I had accepted my solitude. I had accepted the demons that continued to haunt me. I absorbed my flaws and turned them into character defaults. It became a reason not to try, a reason not to wave back at someone that greets you, because, ultimately, you think they are waving at someone else.

Fact: Does anyone really deserve to be hurt by you? Because that's all I ever seem to do to.

I hurt all that I bring in, so I might as well shut them out.

Off the train, up the stairs, and back out onto the street, I hear the clanging of the glass bottle against my leg.

"Just you and me," I said.

Wash it all away. It wasn't going anywhere, but hey, at least gain a reprieve.

I stopped short of the front of my building, checking for clues. There were a few reliable indications whether one of my roommates was home. If the one living in the larger room was home, the window would be slightly ajar (it could be freezing temperatures and the guy still needed the "fresh air"). If the other roommate, the more obnoxious one, was home, the lights would be on. Every single one—hallway, common area, and even in broad daylight, you could tell from street level by the one lamp pressed against the window, namely there because we had no other place to put it. I checked for such details and found none. I was in the clear. That wave of relief, it never gets old. I quietly entered the building, not wanting to cause even the slightest disturbance.

Please no people, please no people, please no people.

A rat, a bunch of roaches, whatever, just no people. I'm rarely this lucky, but I guess the universe throws you one occasionally, always the low hanging fruit, always the shit that doesn't really matter. But I got one that day, and I set down everything, wrote down what I had memorized, freed myself of any obligations, including putting my phone somewhere where I couldn't find it while drunk (also an indication of alcoholic tendencies: knowing how to trick your inebriated self into defending against possible self-sabotage). Last thing I wanted was to call Jiro fifty times, drunk off my ass, like some insane person.

I took my clothes off. It could happen again. I shat myself once, while drunk, and ruined a good pair of pants and the smell, god the smell. I lied to my roommates and said it must have been a dead mouse somewhere. We looked for hours to no avail. Mostly I pretended and did my best not to sweat too much, not to reveal the lie.

Remember, I'm a good liar.

Clothes off, I set out a little placemat of sorts, something around me, where I sat, so any spillage, I could be sure I'd clean up post-haste. The roommates had lives, whole careers. One of them was married and they split time between two apartments. The other had a partner, same kind of deal. They had lives.

"Just a little drinky," I told myself, because who cares—no one was around to hear me.

Just one drink. That's how it starts.

It ends much later, with aching knees, dry mouth, and the sharpest pain in your skull.

And lost time. Don't forget lost time. But I wanted whole patches of time to disappear.

Leave me like all the rest.

Just leave me the bottle, please.

TOURISM

A thought came to mind one morning, while writing through the hangover, a morning free of unfettered and fearful urges: "What if I really am a writer?"

Let me clarify. I had been writing more than ever before. The misery that forced me to the blank page had now become its own breeding ground of guilt. It demanded so much, as you can see in the book you aren't holding in your hands, the book you aren't reading. This book, its sentences became solitary sermons for the self. I was writing so much, I nearly forgot why, the premise of the entire would-be parable.

I had languished in booze and self-loathing for months in attempt to purge and somehow, at the same time, wallow in my failures. While doing so, I rearranged my room to be nothing but a mattress and desk. I had redecorated too. Instead of the various creature comforts like TV and clothes, the stuff bought when you just wanted to buy something, I had stacks of books, many of them I had no idea where I bought, borrowed, or found.

On my desk, a number of empties lined the far side, whereas in the foreground, I had a mug with day-old coffee I still sipped (who cares?), another stack of books, a number of volumes read through, highlighted and marked up with my own handwriting.

I had a chair that I had sweat through, as evidenced in the odor when I plopped down in it.

Everywhere, every surface: layers of dust. The atmosphere of the room was one of absent-minded regret. It looked the part of the person living in their mind.

Nothing about storytelling is ever chronological. I learned by doing, and in admitting to being at best someone needing to write as the only thing I had left, everything took on the luster of letting go. I was letting go of my shame. I was letting go of Jiro.

For a time, I wrote about him as though he were fiction.

Nearly three chapters, I wrote him out of the details. Only later did I begin adding him back in, when I acknowledged the pain it had caused, the falling out my own doing, by design. Like this room, to become the product, I had to run away. I was still running away, it seemed.

I guess my own defeat gave me something to write about.

I had searched so long for something of worth to ink up a page, and now, I had it. You just might have to do what the would-be seasoned writer always says: Write in pain about the pain. Quote lifted from someone. Maybe I made it up. Point being made in every writer's voice on the page is one of desperation, and that desperation comes from the fact that we all have a dream, but seldom do much more than let the dreams linger, eventually fade. In dreaming for actuality, you quickly learn that no one cares. No one cares about your dream, your passion, your art, your science, your goals. You are the one that must care. Dare to do more than that and you just might be successful. I was only beginning to understand what it meant to hurt, to feel the page as much as understand the confines of every paragraph.

My appetite for sushi increased—I would find myself losing focus, scrolling through Seamless at the possible delivery options, adding a Spicy Tuna roll to the cart, only to delete it and add something else. Soon though, both crested into another sort of creativity altogether: the role of the investigator, the sleuth out on the prowl, looking for details lost, and possibly never found. I started gathering together a plan of attack without really fathoming what I was trying to do. In hindsight, it was obvious: I was looking for Jiro. I needed to know, and in some distant way, I hoped I could still apologize.

So you know what I did?

I created a list of restaurants in Manhattan.

Sushi Ko.

Mikaku Sushi.

Blue Ribbon Sushi Izakaya.

Sushi Dojo.

Sushi Azabu.

Sushi Yasuda.

Asuka Sushi.

Tomo Sushi.

Momoya.

Sushi Zo.

I vowed to visit each restaurant. I would do something. What? I hadn't a clue. But I would visit each and by eating there, by appreciating good sushi, I would become closer to Jiro. He would maintain his distance, but in each bite, my being able to explain the flavors, discerning between well prepared and hastily done, I would earn his forgiveness.

I came up with a plan as like what ours had been—similar choices, similar time of day, always at the sushi bar, never in a booth. My notes became part of a search, a faux-detective story. I needed to view it from behind the veil of fiction. I needed more time.

Sometimes everything hurts so much, you just can't help yourself.

So my investigation was one where Jiro went missing. The masterful chef, the man that could make melt-in-your-mouth sushi, he was there and then suddenly he was not. Jiro and his reputable restaurant, his recipes, poof, evaporated: gone fishing.

In this fiction, the documentary existed and was a success. In this fiction, Jiro was back in Tokyo, collecting praise, making sushi, happily affixed to the life he deserves.

In this fiction, I created an uncanny mirror image of reality. Prescient in my prose, I couldn't have thought it to be true.

A thought, though: I could have just texted—I will find out long after I've incurred even more debt from eating at all these restaurants that if only I would have reached out, I would have received both a reply and his forgiveness. If only. The writer in me was hungry for the investigation, and my propensity for delusion added fuel to the already uncontrollable nature to a fire, any fire. He probably waited for me to text him; every day I didn't he grew more disappointed. I'd believe it.

For me to function, I needed to turn myself into fiction.

The city takes on such a curious shape when viewed from behind a magnifying glass. To be fair, my "magnifying glass" was my phone, and my "view" was from behind the very screen I used to hide from others. With purpose clearly in my pocket, right next to the flask full of sake, I was writer turned investigator, searching for a genius gone missing. How cool is that?

"This sushi restaurant won't know what hit 'em," I thought to myself, as I wandered the city wearing not a trench coat or sunglasses, or carrying a gun. I walked in wearing the same thing I always wore, which I realized only upon acclimating to the air-conditioned environment that I might have worn this shirt since yesterday.

Looking both ways to make sure nobody was looking; I pulled at the shirt and took a whiff.

Well, shit. "It all goes downhill from here," I said. In truth, this was just another flicker in an ongoing sequence of events detailing my downward spiral.

It looked like I was having fun, but when the server showed up and asked if I wanted anything to drink, any appetizers, I waited, expecting Jiro to order out of habit. I looked to my left, where he always sat, and there was instead someone else, someone I would never know.

The server tilted her head, "Need more time?"

I became anxious, "Oh, no, umm," I said, flipping through the menu, afraid that if I didn't order now I wouldn't get a second chance. The server would leave and forget me like everyone else. Don't leave me, don't leave me.

My stomach growled. "What would you, umm, recommend?"

Clicking her pen, she asked, "To start with, or as a main course?"

I lied, "I'm a writer and I should tell you that I am looking to write a review about the restaurant and so I ask for recommendations just to give the establishment the best chance possible for a positive review."

Her eyes lit up, "Then you must sample our omakase menu."

I glanced at the menu. Just don't leave me, just don't leave me… I didn't know what I wanted, which is code for help, but her help wasn't the sort I had asked for. Well okay.

I ordered the salmon roe. Right before she walked away, I added, "Oh make that ten."

"Ten?" The confusion clear, and I am aware. *I am aware.* What writer/investigator or as she saw me, what kind of food critic, orders ten pieces of salmon roe?

"Yeah, that should be good."

I'll tell you what writer/investigator does that: A near blackout drunk one, that's what. In a previous scene, one called, earlier this afternoon, I drank two bottles of sake and almost tripped down some stairs when catching the M train. People tried to catch me, a nice kind gesture that I reacted to with malicious intent.

I told that person, "Thanks but no thanks."

Person said, "Asshole."

I shrugged, "Maybe I don't want to be helped."

You could be certain I was slurring my speech.

Back to the investigation—I ordered ten pieces of the sushi I couldn't stand. This was an act of self-destruction. "This stuff is expensive," I muttered. But then again, I wasn't about to worry about the future. I wrote down some notes, remembering what Jiro had said about salmon roe. I gagged just thinking about it. But okay, fine, this is fine. I imagined that GIF with the dog drinking coffee in a house amid flames. Sure enough, when you are as close to the fire as I was, you don't think about the pain. You are already in pain. Pain grows into a numbness and, like in the eye of a hurricane, you cannot feel the danger and destruction that swarms you from all sides. You are calm in the middle, little more than a menu of traumas.

This investigator needed to use the restroom, almost slipping when getting down from my seat. I tried to throw up but nothing came out.

Text message notification: Credit card fraud alert. I answered, Yes, not realizing that meant I agreed that the transaction at the liquor store earlier today wasn't me. The card was frozen.

Now what was I going to do?

I stood at the toilet, in that stall, pants down, not sure what would be my next action.

Well, okay—I would have to call the credit card company but the thought of doing that seemed equally as impossible as the dine-and-dash option floating in my head.

My decision as writer/investigator, as drunk person, was to walk back to the sushi bar and pretend nothing happened. The salmon roe waiting for me as I arrived. I took one look and became nauseous. But I had so much to prove. By eating this, and more so appreciating the flavor of salmon roe, I would be getting closer to Jiro. I will find him through the food he adored.

The server appeared at my side, "How is everything?"

I couldn't speak. I had a piece in my mouth. What came as some surprise was the smooth texture; I expected something different, maybe grainy, the way rice feels in your mouth. I guess I had a strange, distressed look (it's not you, it's me), because the server shook her head, "Our apologies. Would you like to try something else? I highly recommend the omakase menu." She looked at the nine pieces remaining on my plate, "And I will have the chef replace the salmon roe with something special!"

I couldn't swallow, I couldn't speak. Someone else, I guess some bus boy, walked up and proceeded to take my plate. The server chimed in, "Not to worry about this. It's on the house."

Once again, I was getting the easy way out.

Wasn't it always the way—what I feared was swept under the rug.

Not this time. I grabbed at the plate and shook my head. I glared at the bus boy, and then with my other free hand, took the flask from my pocket and downed sake to swallow the sushi. Ugh, I could taste it and imagined the odor on my breath.

"This will be fine," I told the server.

"Sir, are you..."

"Yes I am okay." Whoops, I corrected the slippage, "I mean to say, I'm enjoying the meal."

Freed from their scrutiny, though I tossed in a request for sake, implying if something is going to be on the house, how about the sake? The server didn't protest, "Compliments from the chef!" I did whatever you do to get people to go away.

"This is for you Jiro," I said, lifting another piece to my mouth. I pretended he was close by. Maybe he was in the same restaurant. Sushi Ko had been one of the places we dined at. I remember. Or at least I think I remember. The second piece was just as bad as the first but with warm sake it made it almost bearable.

Just don't think about it sitting in your stomach because it *will* make you throw up.

Third piece wasn't so bad, in that I was able to take it all in with little to no hesitation. By the sixth piece, I didn't need the sake anymore. I was drunk and didn't mind the taste. When the plate was empty, all ten pieces eaten, I exhaled, both relieved that it was over and surprised to admit that it wasn't as bad as I had thought. Everything I fear or dislike, I exaggerate, transforming it into tiny demons, the sort of specimens that keep you from enjoying the moment. It keeps you preoccupied. The server returned and asked if I wanted anything else.

I looked at the empty bottle of sake.

"More sake?"

I grinned, "You read my mind."

Really, who was capable of such a thing, reading minds? Jiro, he could read you and know what sushi to prepare. He never showed it but I am as certain now as I was before of Jiro's incredible observation skills. Jiro, you'll be happy to know that I like salmon roe. Better yet, you'll be happy to know that I'm learning, really learning, about the difference between a meal and an experience.

The server returned with the check.

"Umm," I could sense my body breaking into a sweat, which would make me stink even more than I already did; my body odor would cause me to sweat right through my shirt.

"Not to worry," she grinned, "we comped the sake."

Just smile. I took a gulp of sake.

"I'll be back for the check whenever you're ready!" The server retired to the kitchen.

Jiro, don't look. I was not proud about what I did. No trouble at all, just a quick call to the credit card company and everything would have been okay. Instead I got up and left. I made a scene. I tripped and fell as I ran. My vision a blur, it triggered the memory of the night I ran from the lie, the moment I ran from you. And then I threw up on someone's shoe.

This wouldn't have been the fucked up fictional investigation (read: delusion) I made it out to be if the writer/investigator didn't get beat up, right? I woke up to a familiar pain, a familiar now fading dream, but with one new addition: a broken face. I had been lucky. I only had cuts and bruises, but there had indeed been a fight. No, there had been a fall. In fiction, I will say someone tripped me. In fiction, I will say it was, straight up, a back alley first fight. But I had no one to impart with the telling so it ends up here, on the page, without any clear details, no explanation of my wounded face. I even admit to my inner deception.

I spoke into my tape recorder, my voice sounding terrible, but I had gotten adept at documenting everything. I was so much better now, as a writer. I was writing nearly four thousand words a day. So then after something like last night, beyond dramatization, I noted just how different things felt that morning. I was depressed, but it wasn't in the same way. Not like how I normally dealt with it, the post-physical collision made it difficult to parse thoughts. They just came in, arriving without any filter.

I started thinking about grade school, that time when I wrote down a list of everyone in my class, their real names next to what I called their "nick names." Some delved on funny, others on cool, but most were pure ridicule. Things didn't go down well. Seldom do.

I wrote his name down.

Noted how it made me feel.

Every time I saw his name, it pulled from the ethers something I regret. A person can and will do so much to shield themselves from true feeling. Yet here they were, stinging as freshly as when first thought.

I took another drink. This early? The writer/investigator did not have any need to go anywhere. With less than $50 to their name, the writer/investigator had everything they needed, right here. I had forgotten to hide my phone, and so I did something (uh oh).

I texted Jiro, but I didn't text him apologies. I didn't ask him if he was okay. I didn't even start with a hello. Instead, I texted him the opposite of lies. For once, I texted him truth, no matter how much it hurt to have these words staring back at me.

I texted, "I was a writer first and a friend second. The latter inspired the former and the former often drove away the latter."

I texted, "How miserable must a person be to knowingly spend time with a person. You know you'll one day hurt that person. You know one day your friendship will change. You can only hope it'll be better rather than worse, after you both do a little bloodletting."

I texted, "Take that first impression seriously. First time you meet a person is usually the best chance you got at figuring them out before you are a) too biased to see through the bullshit and/or b) too enamored with what you might get out of them."

I took another gulp and then texted, "That brings me to you. And the confusion you rode in on, I continue to chase after your lead."

I texted, "I lie out of care and out of worrying that I wouldn't be accepted if I were honest."

Then I got a little defensive, "Who actually tells the truth? Who wants to hear the truth? We're all medicating ourselves so that we don't have to hear the truth."

I texted, "When you share a drink with someone, you are doing more than just getting drunk. You are communing in a manner that says the time spent together is worth tempting death, because isn't that what we're doing when attacking our bodies?"

I texted, "That time I did a Google search of you, you had doubted my own lack of a history. I lied and said a lot of things. None of it true, not one bit. I wasn't telling the truth when I said I was a writer. I still don't think I am, but at least now I'm being honest."

I texted, "You were basically homeless but still had a smartphone, still had the means of getting around the city with ease. That's a lot. And props to you for working a job you loathe. I can't even seem to do that."

I texted, "I doubted your own abilities, and especially when I began to hear gossip floating around about you. What I thought was maybe you were as big a fraud as I was. What really was happening was people reacted with jealousy. They knew all about you and feared your talent."

I texted, "Some of the best moments happened during our friendship. No one ever believed in me. But you did. I would go home and learn all about sushi just to try to impress you. It was one of those kinds of bonds where one looked up to the other. I was ashamed of my inferiority at the time but now, I miss it. I guess what I'm saying is you were a mentor to me."

I texted, "So when that disappears, it's like whiplash. You don't really know what to do. I started by walking, but it wasn't like before. You were nowhere to be found. I used to walk to disappear but now I wandered looking for the opposite. It just wasn't going to work. Now I am on an investigation. I have been writing. I don't walk as much anymore. The first time I met anyone becomes the first time I forget all about the others. There's nobody left."

I texted, "I was embarrassed about how much time we spent together. I wondered if it was weird, to be so close to a friend in a non-sexual way. Then I briefly debated my feelings for you. But no, it was always friendship, plutonic, but still—the fact that I doubted it for a second, and then doubted my doubt, it's shameful. Who cares if it was the case? It's not but why did I always have to blot out the curiosity? Why do I always complicate what wasn't so complex?"

I texted, "Central Park that night, I was so nervous of saying or doing the wrong thing I didn't even really listen to what you told me, not all of it anyway."

I texted, "First time we hung out, and you had me front the bill, it really left a bad taste in my mouth. I wondered if it was always going to be this way. In hindsight, haha."

I texted, "When you had me go to Benihana that first time I saw you cook, I was so embarrassed for you. I felt bad because I didn't want to feel that way, and cared more about how I felt in the situation. By being associated with you, by proxy, I was as excruciatingly pitiful as you. I am not proud of this, but here we are. Wait, no, it should be 'but here I am.'"

I added, "Sorry about the typos. Kind of foggy and in a bad way today."

I texted, "50% of the time I think about what became of the documentary. The other 50% I'm busy dreaming up situations where you, being there, and no longer hanging with me, implies that we won. I mean you won. You got what all those douchebags that night were there to give. Invest and impress. Something like that."

I texted, "It does get easier, managing passion, managing to care beyond yourself. I should treat myself better. I shouldn't have run the way I did that night. I bet you expected me to ask this question, so I might as well not even say it now."

I couldn't resist, adding "Okay fine, what happened? Who told you first? Was it the video? I guess I just hope it was wasn't stepped on, that the truth came from my voice to your mind as seamlessly as possible, and not relayed by, I don't know, Garrett."

I texted, "I actually started to believe that maybe you knew all along."

I was never one for impact and brevity, typically rambling when I had the perfect response in the first place, or not saying enough when I should have given a person more. I added, "Did you know? I think you did. You wouldn't have associated yourself with such a loser like me. I have been feeling so sorry for myself, it's so pathetic it's gone all the way back again and is perfectly fine. The pathology of a narcissist is such that they'll feel sorry for themselves without reason. It could be a good day and bam, they'll still feel sorry they forgot to bring an umbrella."

I texted, "I could go on and on and on and I just might. I don't know yet. I'm being honest now, though. See?"

About twenty minutes elapsed since the last text message was delivered. I received no response. I added, "I meant every word." I couldn't take it back now.

I took another sip.

I got back into bed. I made sure to leave the phone, face down, on my desk. I wouldn't be able to reach it. Wide awake, I drank and watched the sun reflect across the room's walls.

I never returned to my restaurant crawl. It was just the one place, Sushi Ko, and I can't show my face there again. The rest I just didn't have it in me to test. The writer/investigator edited out all intents and purposes from the investigation. What really did one have left but to keep going on virtue of, "Sure, why not?" I started waking up at night, spending my hours in twilight, walking without destination from bar to bar. I began selling books to buy more books, selling books to buy more booze. The thought of saving money was simply not a possibility. There was a fire burning all around me and the only way to quell it was with self-destructive tendencies.

The books I bought I didn't read. I bought them, walked them around the city, and then sold them to the same bookstore.

No employee called me out on it because who cares. The writer/investigator became desperate. The writer/investigator began to indulge themselves, so what?

After standing outside Mikaku Sushi, tempting another dine and dash, I ran out of sake in my flask so to the bar I went. Didn't matter which bar, and really I went to the bar two doors down, the bar closest to the restaurant, closest to where I should be. When I leave something behind, I never go very far. I leave the scene of the accident for the view from around the corner. Peering back, I see the world continue without me, acknowledgment that my mistakes are as muted as my best moments.

This is the scene in the investigation where nothing is going right and so the writer/investigator goes to a bar and gets drunk alone among so many others, always alone unless being confronted, and this writer/investigator is not about confrontation.

The bar was busier than expected. I didn't need to be communicating with other people so I walked to the back of the bar, the last seat, the one facing the wall.

Please don't talk to me, please don't talk to me.

The bartender walked up and I barked out my order.

"Warm or cold?"

"I like it warm," I said.

"Bottle?"

I stared at him.

"I'll get you that bottle," the bartender said. Yeah, go to the other side of the bar. This was the part of the investigation where the writer/investigator languished in booze, a sad-sack sort of celebration for all that would never go right.

Yeah, whatever.

"Your sake," the bartender said, placing the warm bottle and glass in front of me.

"Keep it coming."

The bartender opened his mouth to speak but I shut him up. "When this one's empty, replace with a new one. Repeat as desired. And I desire it."

The customer is always right.

I was getting worse—and I could see it happening before my very eyes. I understood just how horrible this bender was on my health, how I indulged in the act rather than examining my anxiety. I guess sometimes you can't help yourself.

Distantly I couldn't stop thinking about how Jiro never responded. He never texted me back. I drank the bottle down without any trouble. Sake always went down smooth. All around me, voices clattering together and I remained distant with my disinterest.

MICHAEL J. SEIDLINGER

The bartender replaced the bottle with another, and I stared at it, never the bartender, eyes trained to the label. Alcohol content 41%. That'll do nicely.

I stuck to a similar pace, gulp, ten second pause, gulp, ten second pause, and by the third bottle, I was feeling pretty good. My mind began to wander. No more thoughts about the documentary, or about Jiro; no more thoughts about the writing that ran in circles, like some enabler, its purpose was to blind me. When the writing was going well, I could almost believe that one day things would level off, that my story had a happy ending. Most days, I write paragraphs and refuse to read them, much like how Jiro probably never read my text messages.

My mind wandered. I thought about the time Jiro and I got drunk and talked about fear. He feared more than just the customer disliking his sushi. He worried that one day the fish would all disappear, no more tuna, and he worried about the carelessness of the general population, preferring material wealth and popularity to any skill or passion. He was on the verge of tears. I had never seen him so visibly upset, and that included the moment on the bridge, the night in Central Park. He was upset then, battling his emotions, but when he talked about the extinction of all things, he gave in. No, he gave up. He let it show.

A eulogy for all that we would lose, we drank in celebration of extinction.

Someone bumped into me. We could stand to have less people in the world.

Really starting to feel it now. I watched people at the bar laughing, enjoying their buzz. This is the part where the writer/investigator morphs into a sad drunk.

My mind wandered. It was swept up by a conversation between two men sitting at a table behind me. One noticeably older than the other, clear from the gruffness of the voice, he spoke to the other man with a tone that said, "You'll get this, just take my advice."

141

"I'm just not sure," the younger man said.

"To be what you desire, you must admit to the desire."

"Yeah," he said, "I guess you're right. But how?"

"By saying, 'I want to be a chef.'"

"I… want to be a chef."

The voice louder, "Mean it."

"I want to be a chef."

"Oh, come on."

"I want to be a chef!"

"It is hard work," the older man scolded, "but there is a dream to be a chef, there is a dream you must carry with you, owning it with every fiber of your being. You cannot just make sushi, or become a factor in someone else's empire. You need to find your own empire. Become more than the average, because if you aspire for the impossible, you will find yourself somewhere unexpected. You may never achieve perfection, I cannot be sure I have, alas, you will wake up one day and understand the gravity of your success."

"How long did it take you to find your way?"

"Enough time that I had become someone else."

"Really?"

"Enough time that I had lost those that had joined me at the beginning."

They weren't strangers.

"Wow."

"I have no reason to ask, for I already know your answer."

I imagined in him the experience and instruction Jiro had given me. In the younger, I conjured the same confusion and doubt that had brought me to him, brought me to tears when I acknowledged that I was the one that he had lost, the one that this old man was referring to. I was the person that stole and contributed to his suffering.

I had tears streaming down my face. People were watching. By people I meant the bartender who broke the silence I required with a question, "Sir, are you okay?"

Nodding, I said, "Yes, tell me how much I have left."

I had enough for a beer, not much else. I waved him off, "Keep the change."

"Are you sure?"

But my mind was already elsewhere. Yes, more wandering.

I wasn't thinking about how I needed that money for the subway. I didn't think about the ordeal just ahead. I was no longer the writer/investigator. It was just me, and I missed my friend.

Walking back home because I couldn't afford the subway, staring at my phone like I always did, I hoped for someone to call. I imagined a number, unrecognized, from New York. I imagined it might be Jiro, calling from somewhere new. I would hesitate at a street corner, unsure of who it might be. I would wait a moment, clear my throat before answering. I didn't need to indulge in the fantasy, no need to stay with it another moment. The screen remained dim, lifeless.

"Do you have time to meet up for lunch, say tomorrow?" Not wanting to jump to conclusions, I say, "Sure, what did you want to talk about?"

His words would be, "I think you already know."

I leave the fantasy; it doesn't easily leave me.

TIME LAPSE

Y ou get your shit together. By "you" I mean me, and my me,
I mean quitting the binge drinking, completely cutting it
from the routine. Not even one sip. And I don't have trouble, either. After a few slipups, self-hating mornings ripe with hangover, I found my footing. I mean putting a roadblock to the collision
course of self-destruction I had been steering across the city for what
seemed like weeks. It could have been months. I mean quitting the
delusion, the writer/investigator sendoff. I saw from outside the path
I had been walking. I saw the same footprints, faded splatters of vom-
it, torn pages from the book that even the wind had refused. They
remained, rain-soaked and pasted to the pavement. The last thing I
wanted was to see blood splatter, or worse, my broken body slumped
over a park bench.

Grief holds you down, but eventually you wrestle free.

Less is more, so I will choose to be less.

Like waking up for the first time, I was confused—absolutely
stunned by how much of my room was in disrepair. The mattress
propped to one side with the sheets tied in knots like a makeshift
rope, having no recollection of doing so, not to mention the books

145

stacked to be a pyramid, the lone book not a part of the whole being a guide to card stacking. Yeah, I think had the technique, just lacking in application. Probably needed a deck of cards.

Save for waking up to a partial-manuscript completed, I was, as one might say, completely displaced. What the hell happened?

I read through what I had been written, and got to the "investigation" and had enough. I had no recollection of those pages. In their stead, I had only a few half-formed thoughts, and the sinking feeling that I was missing something, a tourist to such treacherous thoughts.

Written in sharpie on a hardcover of a Paul Auster novel was a list of sushi restaurants: Sushi Ko, Mikaku Sushi, Blue Ribbon Sushi Izakaya, Sushi Dojo, Sushi Azabu, and so on. They were all misspelled, and written in near illegible handwriting. It was undoubtedly mine, but I still couldn't believe how much I let myself get away with.

I retraced every step, and found myself facing Manhattan Bridge, slightly flopsweat, the sudden realization that I could finish this book. I could finish this book and it didn't need to hide behind a fictional narrative. I could finish this book and perhaps in doing so, I would still meet Jiro again. For once, it wasn't my sole motivation. The book, first and foremost. I wanted to be able to write the words, "The End." Writing them just might close the door on this era of my life.

Doubtful but this was my thought-process going into the clean-up of the mess that was my life. Time passed with every item repaired, stack of books returned and reclaimed to their rightful position, the mattress tossed (these would be the sleeping bag days), and even though my credit cards were maxed, I managed to reconsolidate and lower the monthly payments.

Fit in another development: I found a job.

All those days of wandering the city, what I never looked for was a job. Wouldn't you know it: It found me. The one thing I probably needed to survive, the one thing so many people search tirelessly for and it just found me.

I spent my 9–5s like a good employee. Everyone needed someone to put data in an Excel spreadsheet, type up notes and reports for people that talked too quickly so you had to keep rewinding the audio clips, often having to "figure out" what hadn't made sense in the first place.

I went to happy hour with the colleagues and drank seltzer, took part in conversations, and I mean really be part of the conversation, not just sit there and laugh when everyone else laughed. I even went to one of the guys' cookouts, one of those flings that take the entire Saturday afternoon and you stand around in the sun, burning, watching people drink cheap beer and maybe eat a hot dog. I went all the way to Queens for that one.

I started dating someone from the office, casually, or at least it was for me. Some nights we'd stay up all night talking and in those late/early hours I almost didn't recognize that it was me, that this was my life. It wasn't just a peck on the cheek.

Sometimes a body yearns but the mind, it doesn't ever let you forget.

I spent Friday nights writing—it's Friday night as I type this very sentence—and it was the only part of the week where I could count the minutes, tallied up in two-hour long increments. It became sanctuary, and during those first weeks on the job, it saved me from turning once again to the bottle. There was a liquor store a block away in every direction. I was working, paying off my credit card debt; I even had money left over after paying rent. How awesome was that?

I didn't walk the city anymore. I didn't want to be found.

I didn't eat sushi. Food was for filling the stomach. My appreciation for each meal extended to how long I would have to wait until the food had been prepared.

Routine as life, life as routine: One day the office scheduled a lunch junket at, of all places, Benihana. Mere mention of the place sent my mind careening back to the long nights where Jiro and I recorded footage of him practicing making sushi. It sent me back to the teppanyaki grill, head down, just in case he saw me, or maybe Garrett. I didn't say a word, ate the food I ordered, kept my mouth shut, basically became the person I had been before getting this job.

You bet they noticed. Questions like, "What's wrong with you?" and "Are we boring you?" were peppered with cause for concern, insincere, but still, a cause: "You okay?" someone whispered, "get yourself together. You don't want to be stuck an assistant forever."

That's just it—I didn't care. I excused myself from the discussion, whatever it was they were talking about, and took the long way to the restrooms in the back. For every face I did not recognize, the lazier I became with hiding mine. Reaching the restrooms, I turned on the balls of my feet, no reason to keep up the charade.

I walked up to the maître d and asked, "By any chance, is Garrett in?"

That all-too-familiar fake restaurant hospitality, smiling and showing teeth, she told me in an apologetic tone that he was "taking some time off." I'll admit that hearing this sent a chill down my spine. Further inquiries came up empty, "Would you like to leave him message? I'll be sure he gets it." My mind raced about all kinds of possibilities—why would Garrett be taking time off? He never took time off. Never, even if he was sick. He would sleep in the back of the kitchen but he would still be at this stupid fucking restaurant. Did something happen after that night? From one to the next, I imagined Garrett tending to Jiro—as his manager, as his executor of estate, as his confidant. I couldn't stop thinking about it. I asked one of the sushi chefs, and one seemingly recognized me, "You're Jiro's friend."

Looking over my shoulder, back at the table, catching a few of my colleague's glares, it looked bad. I was fucking up, fucking it all up. Could see the whole routine breaking apart, and yet, I kept on, "Yeah, have you seen him lately?"

Instead of returning to the table, I leaned forward, sat at the sushi bar and listened, nearly begged for details. It wasn't conclusive, but the chef told me about Garrett's whereabouts.

"He's on vacation," the chef said as he sliced some akami, "West Coast. Other side of the country. The guy needed it after all that."

I could feel my entire body shaking but, I needed to know.

"Did something happen?"

"Oh yeah, it was a whole production."

"Production?" My fears and fantasies were coming to fruition.

"Yeah," he offered me a piece of sushi.

I glanced down at it. My first thought being, Jiro would not have approved. He would have taken one look at it and pin pointed the inherent flaw: too many flavors. Did this thing really need chipotle mayo *and* a drizzle of wasabi mayo?

"Garrett bought a restaurant, whole big production. People here were not happy. We feared for our jobs. He's sticking around though. New management. Scary to think, but it is likely."

Before I could ask, he had my answer, "I haven't seen Jiro though. Not for a long time. Some people here miss the guy. He made the best food. I used to eat the leftovers off customers' plates. It was so good. Wasn't much behind the grill, but that's why I make sushi. I don't flip knives. That shit's dangerous."

The guys from the office walked over, walked right past me. Clearly what I had done was a faux pas. I'd find out later some of the people in attendance were on the board of directors. This lunch was a big deal. My feeling is if it really were a big deal, you wouldn't go to Benihana.

I don't lose my job, though I called in sick two days in a row and the third I no-showed. The week nearly done, there wasn't much point in showing up on a Friday. So I didn't. By the time Monday came rolling along, I was already spending every ounce of energy trying to find Garrett.

I went back to Benihana and pretended to be a customer. No, scratch that—I was a customer. I sat at the sushi bar, looking at everyone that passed. Eventually someone noticed me and asked. No, I wasn't an investigator. Word is still out on whether I'm a writer. I was there as myself, a person looking for their friend. I was someone at the bar, doing their damnedest not to order an alcoholic beverage.

The fact that I could, that was always what got me. I could push away the free drinks from others, the beer during an afternoon excursion, the offer to pay for my drinks during a post-work day happy hour, but sitting at a bar or restaurant, especially when I was alone, became almost impossible to *not* do what everyone else did with ease—flag down a bartender and say the words. Just say the words. My words, on that day, were far different than the usual "Jameson on the rocks."

I flagged one of the servers down and asked, "Is Garrett in?"

Be as polite as possible. Don't come off as desperate. Worse, don't come off as depressed.

I asked simply, not at all like some thug from an organized crime syndicate. People asked to see the manager all the time. And not only to complain about the food (I could joke about how the food had gone downhill since Jiro's disappearance).

Off he went, and then I asked one of the sushi chefs, the one wearing a red sash, knowing well my inquiry was a disturbance.

"Do you know Jiro?"

The other chef, the one with glasses, turned to me and said, "A smart man."

Red sash never looked me in the eye, preferring to speak between the slicing of what appeared to be saba, "He hasn't been around."

"He taught me how to better marinade tako," said glasses, with a grin.

"He told *me* I'm proof of how low the bar for culinary professionalism has been set."

Laughter from glasses, who slapped red sash on the shoulder, "You are the bar."

Shaking his head, red sash drizzled wasabi mayo on the maki he had nearly completed, "That's what he said."

Laughing even louder now, glasses shook his head, "Wow, 'culinary professionalism.'"

"Yeah," I interjected, "do you know if he's around?"

The server returned, "It would appear Garrett has taken a leave of absence. Would you like to speak to one of the other managers? Kenneth is right over there." I followed the server's gaze to a man standing with hands in his pockets, looking right at me.

Clearing my throat, "Ahem, no, that'll be alright." I caught myself nervously tapping my fingers on the counter. Enough of that. "I think I'll just have a quick bite and I'll be off."

The server stood around unsatisfied until being called back to one of the teppanyaki tables. Now was my chance. I asked the chefs, opting for honesty—you know, a friend, worried sick, wondering what happened, haven't heard from him in weeks, no reply to my texts or calls. The one with the red sash said, "You sound like a jilted ex or some shit."

Glasses sighed, "No one knows. But there was someone asking the same recently."

"Oh yeah?" I said, "so my worries are for real?"

"He left a card," the chef said, fumbling around, "I tossed it aside. Could still be here."

"What are you, some investigator?" asked red sash.

Funny how you should mention it… "No, just a writer and Jiro's friend."

"A writer," red sash placed a piece of sashimi on a plate, "there are so many of you." Regarding the sushi, red sash nodded, "For a missing friend."

Glasses handed me the business card, "You're in luck."

"I can take this?"

Shrugging, glasses said, "No use to me."

It was the least I could do: I ordered a full meal and doused most of it in soy sauce to conceal the flavor. It wasn't that the sushi was inadequate, far from it; rather, my tastebuds have known the lengths with which such a savory depth of flavor could be produced using these very same ingredients. The chefs kept mostly to themselves, but the one with the glasses acknowledged me upon departure, "Good luck, dude." I waved and said, as solemnly as possible, "Thanks."

The name on the card—it floored me, left me frozen in the wind. Literally, I was the person stopping traffic on the sidewalk, the idiot everyone cursed silently or stopping dead in their tracks. A few nudges, maybe one guy calling me out, "Move, asshole!" But the name, the name on the card:

It was Nolan's.

Sheer panic followed by a dizzying sequence of half-thoughts— why would Nolan be looking for Jiro? Does this mean my nightmare isn't true? Does it mean it's worse? Does this mean Jiro really disappeared, from everyone's lives? That empty feeling you have right as you are reminded of a betrayal, followed by the horror of the remembrance it was your own doing. What if Jiro killed himself? I understood that it wasn't unreasonable to have such a thought. Flashes of that rainy afternoon on the Manhattan Bridge. The now distant sound of his voice as he confessed to me how vulnerable he felt, how hitting rock bottom, you think it couldn't get much worse. The very bottom is merely a benchmark for how much further you've got to fall.

Yeah, I made the call. Made sure to be in a room alone, as if anyone around me would care; it had more to do with vulnerability. He picked up on the third ring. Sounding a little lethargic, "Hello…?" I returned the hesitance, "Nolan…?"

A breath, followed by silence. My voice must have sounded familiar. I would have to make the first move.

"I'm calling about Jiro."

He snapped, "I know why you're calling. You really fucked things up. But you know that already huh?"

Admitting is the first step to acceptance.

"I know." I should have said something more but the words did not come. Where there had once been countless digressions, I had only the sound of my voice leaving me.

"Yeah? You knew and yet here we are."

"I know," I said.

"Whatever," he sighed, "you really fucked him up. But even losers like you can't hold down a star as bright as Jiro from continuing to shine."

Might as well come out and say it. "Is Jiro okay?"

"He is, now."

"And…"

Sure I had lied but in the deception I discovered so much about myself.

"And you won't ever know where he went. We all agreed, for Jiro's sake, not to surround him with negative influences."

I was silent, speechless.

What does one say when the last life in them is squashed, when even a "goodbye" is nullified by the voices of those that had your number, had your demons all figured out?

"But I will give you this—you're not that bad of a writer. The stuff you filmed, pretty good. I particularly like all the food porn. Jiro really trusted you. It takes a lot to get someone comfortable behind the camera, especially with regards to the most vulnerable of subjects: themselves."

What was he getting at?

"Thankfully, there wasn't much to repair."

"You mean…" Stricken, my hands shook, my eyes closed, maybe never again to reopen. I had fallen my knees. Where there should be tears, there was instead nothing. I was about as far removed from being a functioning human being as possible. This was what you called the individual in hell.

"Yeah, the documentary is cut—has received highly positive re-actions from the handful of critics and culinary experts that have seen it. We're submitting it for film festivals across the country. Big, big, big—thinking big."

"Jiro deserves it…"

Nolan laughed, "You sound upset."

"I am not," I said, lifelessly.

"Whatever, anyway, sorry I can't help you."

Nolan hung up. What first came to mind, as I sat, and then laid there on the floor, the most selfish of thoughts: They stole my work and claimed it as their own. Nolan erased my name and branded it as his. Though I may have committed fraud, don't I still have the right to be credited?

No, stop, enough of that. Jiro—he was alive. Better yet, Jiro may very well be better off, without me, without anyone to bring him down. For that reason alone, I would be okay. Jiro would be remem-bered. It's okay. It's all okay now.

I dropped the phone and repeated it to myself.

"I'll be okay."

"I'll be okay."

I'll be okay.

FOR YOUR
VIEWING CONSIDERATION

*T*here are two versions to any truth, and here I will give first the hopeful and then the actual, the latter of which I learn through the confidence of Jiro's investors, long after grief rendered me worthless. Jiro was okay and that information sustained me against everything.

I imagine it all in the framework of a film, my film, or rather as it shall be known by all: Nolan's film. No, fuck that, it was Jiro's, it was his from the beginning.

There's a piece of sushi being formed—from the initial touch of the blade, to the adding of the vinegared rice, and finally to the delicate gesture of the brush, dipped in soy and lightly brushed across the topping. The soy causes barely a drip. The seasoned professional responsible for this amazing display, it turns out is Jiro.

We hear his voice, "What defines deliciousness?" Closeup of a weathered face, Jiro's, as he considers the camera, conceivably one of our countless interviews, "Once you decide on your occupation, you must immerse yourself in your work. You have to fall in love with

155

your work. Never complain about your job. You must dedicate your life to mastering your skill. That's the secret of success and is the key to being regarded honorably."

Return to the preparation and eating of sushi, always return to the sushi.

It's precisely as Jiro would have wanted. Sprinkled throughout would be the systematic portrayal of process, the preparation followed by the meal itself, complete with the footage I had filmed that night, that fucking night, ugh.

Jiro never revealed all his secrets, but in this fantasy, anyway, he does—enough to explain how to best prepare and serve the rice— room temperature, *not* cold—the part about massaging the octopus for hours, which will always resonate deeply with me, for it brought our friendship to a new level. Eighteen pieces of sushi total, including the meal-ender, grilled egg, would be featured alongside the luminous footage of each ingredient given the attention and care it deserves.

It would be filmed in such a manner that one could imagine Jiro was in any city, creating a sense of hope that might be lost on all viewers but Jiro and I, an inside joke rendered entirely for ourselves, fellow wayward walkers of such a lonely city.

As per Jiro's request, details of his past would be kept to a minimum. Less to do about the journey and more about what has consumed his days. Sensitive topics such as parents, children, marriage(s), and suicide exist solely to shape the inner turmoil that has defined the shadow Jiro casts, but ultimately, the passion with which he has devoted his life to a craft, the passion that resounds and rings true, striking a chord in anyone seeking a life defined not by worldly possessions but in tireless practice. He had a name for it, shokunin. The shokunin puts work first, wants nothing more than to be immersed in the peculiarities of their craft.

This was not a documentary detailing Jiro's downfall. It is not a complex film. Its purpose is to praise, to shine a single, solitary light on someone whose work had got largely unnoticed.

The sushi itself is simple, the depth of flavor tapping into a purity that cannot be taught. It takes practice, decades of daily repetition, to extract understanding from an unknown.

Cue the image of Jiro washing his hands, conceivably at a prime moment post preparation. Again to his hands, both showing their age, the skin stretched and thin to show a web veins, the skin itself a story, each wrinkle a moment of sadness and suffering. He washes them clean.

Another scene, he is where he always is, in the chef's position, footage from a particularly dejected evening, when we had both too much to drink, the drinking itself spurred on by a discussion that depressed us both.

Image of Jiro flicking seaweed against a grill, the open flame heating and accurately inducing more of a flavor and crunch to the ingredient.

"I would much rather die knowing that I have come to understand something more than when I had initially set out on this strained venture." Jiro's words echoing over the footage, each frame over-exposed because I hadn't a clue what I was doing at the time. But the words, they could only be his. Only Jiro spoke with such magnitude. Every statement was from a reservoir of experience, each line chiseled from the very act of denial that had been much of his life.

There is a reason he is unknown, and the decision was not his. An interlude depicting the struggles, homelessness, and yes, implication of his own work being stolen from him (seeing a thread here, and for that I will forever be sorry).

And then over an image of Jiro at the bridge that afternoon, the words repeat, "You must immerse yourself in work."

A pause, followed by the image of Jiro on the verge of breakdown, "Always try to improve upon yourself." Even when you can feel it in your bones, the threat of collapse near, try because there is nothing you can do better than to continue each attempt.

Jiro taught me this, and eclipsed by loss, I am now beginning to understand.

It would then alternate between footage taken at the fish market and one of our citywide walks. The density of these shots, particularly the captured footage from the market, work to counterbalance each other, where the content involving our walk is far more concealing, more considerate of the viewer. It gives them some breathing room between the onslaught.

The voiceover comes in so seamlessly it's as though from another universe: "Some have a sensitive palate and sense of smell. That's what you call natural talent. In this line of business, if you take it seriously, you'll become skilled. But if you want to make a mark in the world, you have to have talent. The rest is how hard you work."

I never filmed the sea or anything like that but I imagine there needs to be something in the way of seeing the very thing we are consuming, in its natural habitat. We need to see fish being fish, flowing with and against the current, the blue of the sea counteracted against the darker depths, just beyond what is filmable.

An aside, discussion about overfishing and the bastardization of sushi. Jiro's belief that the muddying of the recipe, the overproducing of conveyor belt sushi, faux-creations demanding more fish, is a natural reaction to the rise in popularity of the cuisine. Yet the dilution hurts more than just the artform; it destroys the ecosystem.

The passion is reproduced onscreen.

In every line and every frame, I hear only Jiro's voice. This isn't a documentary, it's Jiro's declaration of a life endured for the sake of sushi.

In the second version, it is what I have come to expect. Certainly, some of this I gather from Nolan and the piecemeal investigation I had poorly enacted for reasons that involved another misstep into self-destruction. But the facts are facts and the documentary is completed, director credit given to someone else; funding for Jiro's restaurant is secured, and the reason why I hadn't seen Jiro in these streets is because he no longer walks them. Garrett ensures that Jiro returns home. There is talk between investors about safe passage, but inevitably Jiro returns and faces his demons. As ever an inspiration, he does the unthinkable: He forgives his son. I cannot imagine the amount of restraint and self-reflection required to forgive someone that has single-handedly set you back two and a half decades of work. (What if he doesn't forgive me?) The son continues operating the restaurant. Jiro opens his own, conceivably to some success. The differences in menu are substantial, especially where interests are concerned, his son begins to explore maki and other means of specialty rolls whereas Jiro continues making the simple yet ample omakase to which his life had been devoted. A lot changes, maybe not as much as I would expect; however, it is enough to feel as though the future is far better than any present Jiro and I had shared.

I remain in the present tense, unaware of what has already come to pass.

I remain in the fantasy, because it is all I have.

But even a fantasy will have to come to an end. A conclusion so concussive, the viewer would demand the happiest of endings. Instead, I would see it from one artist to another, knowing well that in Jiro he deals as much in devastation as he does with the next destination. In his journey, he is never standing still, always traveling closer to a new definition. The fantasy ends with Jiro riding the train, an expression typically sullen and straight.

But just when you think it's going to fade to black, Jiro considers the camera and cannot hold back his smile, as if to imply he has lived a full life. He has no regrets.

BEING

My own confession, which has taken me so long to write, goes something like this:

I just wanted to be a writer.

He just wanted to be a chef.

The difference is one had succeeded while the other got caught up in dreams of being, but never thought to look past the dream. I never thought to look at myself.

See what anyone else sees.

I'm sorry, Jiro, but you've found your way. You have reached the next destination.

How ironic, when you finally called me, I thought it was my imagination. When you called, I couldn't pick up the phone. All ten rings before the screen once again dimmed, the notification, 1 missed call from "Jiro." Maybe we will meet again, but I need to be better. I can't talk to you as the same person; you would demand of me more.

There was a price to be paid for dreaming, and I had not yet named mine.

OUT TO PASTURE

With my last bit of savings, I left the city. A break, not a move, though who would have noticed my departure? A friend from high school reached out and asked if I would be up for house-sitting for a few months. He had both quite the house and quite the dog in need of constant assurance and affection. The dog was a rescue, carrying trauma from enduring something untold. Never mind the fact that I hadn't heard from John in at least a decade. I accepted the offer because of the dog. Fuck it, I accepted the offer because nothing else was working for me in the city. Maybe when I returned, I could once again be treated as new blood for the vampires feasting on the city's social circles.

Not until I walked those streets, took that maybe last subway ride (oh who was I kidding) to the airport, and was in the air, so far up in the clouds, did I understand just how much I needed the space. I could feel it in my bones, the dull ache you get used to ignoring, much like you get used to disappointment, those days full of nothing but allaying the spare dream you keep hidden among the demons in your closet.

The Uber ride to the house, I kept trying to talk to the driver, but the driver would give me one word answers. "Yeah." "True." "I feel that." I was nervous. Surrounded by landscapes of death, the desert full of brown, almost reddish dirt, the beauty by design made to dupe those into comfort, but I was too smart. I used to feel the same way when I saw the city's beautiful skyline at night.

This was a place where dreams are made.

Something about an opportunity, and the feeling of belonging.

Youth does that, not to say I'm that much older. I just maybe felt like it. Time morphs and changes its conditions so much I couldn't tell a person how long it's been since the last time I cared about keeping up with it.

How many news cycles does it take for a person to lose themselves in the details?

The house was as beautiful as the clouds, and designed to reflect it. Paneled windows across the entire front and back, this was the stuff serial killers were made of. At night, the person with sinister intentions waiting outside, watching everything happening indoors, the entire house like a glass enclosure for future victims.

Yeah, I wasn't above such negative thoughts. I laughed it off and tipped the Uber guy extra for being a dick. Maybe I deserved to be alone right now.

Don't entertain this person, they need time to heal, to think.

That's what I spent most of my time doing at the house.

Darcy, the dog, a sad little pug, was my sole responsibility, and the routine defined itself around every meal and walk. She never barked, mostly sat in one of three locations in the house, paced around. Darcy never spoke, favoring instead to express herself by crying.

I sat with her, petting her head, rubbing her stomach, watching her drift off to sleep, while I silently shed some tears too. It didn't last more than a week before the routine was up eight in the morning sharp, every morning, a mile long walk into nowhere, kicking up dirt, getting underneath the nailbeds of each finger; back to the house to hydrate and lounge, reading a few chapters, go into town twice a week, which meant paying for an Uber, to check out more books from the library, gather up some groceries, and enjoy coffee at a diner across from the lone pub open mid-day, just to test myself, to prove that I no longer craved a sip. Around four in the afternoon, after a heavy meal, Darcy and I walked the same route, only instead of taking a left at the fork in the trail, we took a right and enjoyed the sunset from a minor ledge in the otherwise unpredictable desert. With the last remnants of sunlight, drenched in dark orange, we navigated our way back to the house for dinner, a movie, and to dose off to a book. On the occasion that I could, I would write.

When I wrote, it poured out, whole episodes, the words that should have been mine but truth be told they were given to me, a means of penance for every past embellishment. There was truth in those pages, though I would turn away from them more often than I would reread, edit, and understand how this was supposed to end. I guess I wanted it to end differently, with more of the past restored. But that's life, and every expectation existed to be underestimated.

The silence in the desert, it became the music of every moment. The speakers on my laptop remained mute, and I almost never logged into social media, or checked the internet. It helped that the house didn't get a great signal in all respects, including phone reception. It was truly a place of disappearances, and at night, after Darcy had plummeted into a heavy sleep, I would sometimes sit outside on the deck, in the cold, and watch my breath, pretending it was cigar smoke. In each rock, each square inch of dirt, there was a story, and I wrote them in my mind, tales of peoples' final steps, resting places, the point in a life where the franticness of the beating heart slowed, becoming acceptable. You could take a break, the place seemed to say. A life could be so much clearer and simpler, if you stopped busying yourself with the possibilities and instead focused on what's possible. Exhale a plume and like a prayer. I closed my eyes and said, "Maybe someday."

Every time I would ask myself, "What would Jiro do?" WWJD. Like some stifling mantra, what would he have done, in this situation, with this sentence, with *my* story?

The theoretical conversation, that same way about his texting where it was always half sentences, always quick, successive to my more belabored, thought-out, less confident rejoinders.

"And what will an artist do with all this time?"

You know a person long enough to ruin their life, it becomes second nature to hear their voice haunt your own mind. Those spare moments lengthened into long spells, and Jiro, don't you know it, I have been writing, really writing.

"To what outcome?"

Did it matter? I was writing, and really I haven't stopped. In each sitting, I saw sentences form before my very eyes. Like the routine here in the desert, sometimes I would sleep right through it, eyes open but mind and meaning glazed over. Still, many would form to find the spare few that get to stick around. Erasure became the essence of my craft.

"Perhaps you are discovering the conditions unique to your own work."

I am, and I couldn't be any more confused, but I've accepted the confusion. I think it was what you said, Jiro, about how you need to immerse yourself in work. If you're going to do that, you will feel smothered, confused, and maybe even lonely. Separation anxiety born from the uprooting of every pillar of your comfort zone. I'm doing just that.

"You'll face innumerable challenges—much of what you believe in will be under threat of being broken."

W.W.J.D.?

I was always a nervous and shy person, never really putting my own beliefs, my own creations, my own attempts out there with confidence. I never really put myself out there at all. But I need to if I'm going to be able to speak. I must if I want to move past the part of being erased. Right now, I'm fine with it, I need to work through some things and I can't do that if I'm busying myself with other demands. It's okay to step aside. One day I'll have a turn. I say all this as much to anyone as I do myself. I'm working on it.

"You are smart, and clever. Keep at it and you'll become the writer you desire."

What else could someone say to that? I would say thank you once, and then thank you again, the second time sincere, emotions brimming to the surface in the form of face blushing and the usual swelling of tears in the eyes. But I wouldn't cry, just like this wouldn't happen.

It's not supposed to. If I have learned anything from what's happened, it was that I had to accept what I had done. There's no taking back what I did. It all remains in disrepair.

"How are you?"

Outside, it was yet another lightless night. The voice echoing throughout the house, not Jiro's, was my own. As it has been, and as it continued to be, those months of pause, sitting in and tending to a house and its history.

On one of my excursions into town, I came across a fresh market that sold and specialized in, for me, a special brand of nostalgia. The word "organic" was a refrain, every other aisle, it seemed like they had to remind customers their tomatoes and carrots and spinach were organic, the chicken, cage free farm fresh, the meats, though still butchered to all hell, were "locally raised."

In the desert? Really.

I perused the aisles and absentmindedly gathered soy, rice, cream cheese, the makings of what would become something very different for me. They had sushi-grade fish, and soon I went from examining the packages, checking the label, lightly squeezing the cuts of meat from behind the veil of shrink-wrap, and added it to my cart.

This was about stepping outside of my comfort zone, right?

As though I had planned on it from the start, I had everything I needed, including the little things, stuff I would have normally forgotten, like, you know, *chopsticks*. Oh and vinegar, which, like soy, wasn't exactly a "little thing."

The whole ride back, I held the grocery bags close, as if the driver cared, who I was pretty sure was the same driver that picked me up before. Maybe the same driver that always picked me up. I was single-handedly providing the guy supplemental income. There went my overactive imagination again, dreaming up a scene where the guy parked just out of view of the house and waited for me to call an Uber. Turn of the ignition and bam, he would be there in a minute.

I never did have a problem calling a car from the desert…

That night, after feeding Darcy, after walking in the near-dark from a stranger than usual sunset (we should have had another 20 minutes, oh well), I started setting the counter with each ingredient. I examined every cut of fish, tuna, salmon, and crab meat. This wasn't going to be a full course. I would have been happy achieving just the one.

Rice cooker, pour the rice, set the time. I used the duration it would take to cook the rice to marinade the tuna, smoke the salmon as I had remembered from watching Jiro. I took out the seaweed, mulled over how I would tend to it. At some point, I began to understand why I was bothering to make sushi at all. This wasn't to impress anyone; rather, each cut piece of tuna, I labored over with the shaky hand of an amateur. This was an absent declaration. I made sushi in some small way to be closer to Jiro, if only in theory.

I set the tuna down in plastic containers of soy sauce. This, I wasn't quite sure if it was as intended, and yet, I wasn't about to look up a set of instructions. There would be no cook book at my side, not on this night, which ironically was the only night I cooked for myself. Routinely I ate salads haphazardly tossed, sandwiches that were exclusively peanut butter and jelly or cold cuts, usually roast beef or salami, with pepper jack cheese, maybe chipotle mayo, maybe nothing at all, as dry as my sense of humor.

The salmon I cooked on a grill. Admittedly I went a step too far, doing more than merely getting that smoky, cooked exterior. "Strike one," I mumbled.

I did not have fresh wasabi, though the label on the package said it was. Good enough for me though. Tuna marinating, salmon fully cooked (oops), seaweed (yeah I wasn't sure what I could do with it) left at room temperature, I waited on the rice. I became tempted to skim a few how-to guides on sushi but, thankfully in my moment of weakness, the house didn't have any internet.

Surprise, surprise, internet blackout.

When the rice was cooked, I did exactly as Jiro had explained— the pouring of the vinegar, just enough to bind and add taste to the sticky rice—and I used a plastic serving spoon to meld them together, emulating the diagonal angle of combing through the rice up and down, for minutes nonstop. A calm washed over me, and I let go, no longer counting the minutes, instead listening to the rice itself for signal of when it was adequate.

And when that happened, I set the seaweed out, "Strike two." Jiro would have raised an eyebrow upon seeing the choice to make maki rather than the far more sophisticated, far more delicate flavors of sashimi. But it was enough for me to correctly roll the ingredients together.

One roll was tuna, with a smearing of cream cheese, which I must say the marinating it in soy for what must have been thirty minutes was an excellent, highly tasty, choice.

But I also adore soy sauce so…

The other, well, there was no other. The salmon became its own entrée, rice on the side, soy for dipping (the salmon was a little dry), and the crab meat, I forgot all about it. It had remained to the left of my makeshift preparing station.

"That's a strike three," I said, looking down at a now completely awake Darcy.

Holding the package of crab meat, I ran through a series of choices, the most popular being to save it for a different meal. Who was I kidding: I wasn't going to do this again. The other was to give it to the dog. Could you serve crab to a dog? The internet down, no means of searching for an answer, I opted for the former, which could have been amended to "leave in fridge and forget about it until establishment of weird smell."

There you had it. Table setting and plating aside, which I took a little bit of artistic license, half-assing the arrangement to fit the meal-for-one scenario. But, yeah, there you had it.

Darcy followed me from kitchen to dining "room," eager to have a taste.

"You're probably better off not sampling this," I said.

The dog let out a single, high pitched whine.

"Yeah, you and me both."

Jiro would not be proud of the result, but I settled into a meal I made with pride knowing well that he would have been astonished by the effort. Sometimes you get so caught up trying ot meet the expectations of others, you forget meeting the most important set of standards: your own. And hey, the tuna wasn't all that bad. Brushed with soy drenched ginger, and it could almost be restaurant acceptable. Almost.

Still, that night, after eating, I paced around the house for a bit, anxious like one would be waiting in the emergency room for a diagnosis.

The verdict here was: stomach, are you going to accept the meal or are we going to have one of those nights spooning porcelain toilet while fending off spasms and tremored heaving?

An hour in, relief: no upset stomach, none of that noxious burping and harsh stomach acid, symptoms of food poisoning. I sat down on the couch, picked up the most recent book, but couldn't concentrate so I turned on the television. Nothing really on, but when was there ever?

I skimmed V..O.D, typical selection, many I either had seen or simply had no interest in viewing. You know how it just creeps up on you, not the stomach pains but the literal loss of balance? One second you're normal and then suddenly you can't seem to catch your breath. The room spun to the sound of classical music, and the familiar voice, with a proposition:

"What defines deliciousness?"

Darcy climbed onto the couch, sat on my lap, looked up at me. A whine caught my attention, huh? Okay, it was okay. This was a good thing. I nuzzled the dog, regained my composure, the surprise wearing out, replaced with sincerity.

I watched the trailer. In watching the trailer, I was meeting Jiro again, as if we had met in a different life and only now, upon seeing the documentary in its full state, I was meeting Jiro the same way everyone met Jiro: through his passion for sushi.

Yet I alone held a secret, something special: Once upon a time I met someone named Jiro, who told me his story, a climb to the top and a shaky fall to the very bottom. His passion never disappeared, even though he did from life, to be reborn and renewed. The passion onscreen did not pale in comparison to the passion I had known. He cared most about sushi, and you could see it in every single shot. Much to my delight, they retained most of my camera work. I could still see my hand in the production. The choice of setting it to the musical work of Philip Glass and Tchaikovsky, made sense. Jiro had always said the preparation and production of sushi was akin to other art forms.

When you were deep in the moment, it was like music.

No wonder during some of my darkest moments, I preferred silence.

The grief does not pass you by. You live long enough, you get to be the one that does the passing. You walk right to the beginning again, able to look right at what once hurt so much, with renewed sight. You're able to lay down on a couch, the warmth of a caring pet at your side, and watch it all happen before your very eyes. It's almost worth it. Almost.

HELLO, MY NAME IS

*I*was putting the finishing touches on a chapter when I received a call. Kind of took me by surprise because the house had undergone a record blackout, no reception or phone signal for nearly a week. The call, it was a 646 area code, unknown number. No I didn't pick up the phone expecting it to be Jiro. The yearning, foolish expectation, had long since passed. But I also didn't expect Garrett to be calling me after, how long has it been?

Those were my first words, "How long has it been?"

"Hey, hey," he said, voice muffled by nearby noise. I imagined a busy city street, taxicabs blaring their horns, the anguished rushed steps of the many venturing to the next step in their nonstop, breakneck careers. "Been real long."

"I bet," I said, unsure of where this is going.

"I got long hair now, that's how long it's been kid."

Kid? But okay, I played along. "Long enough that you're suffering what sounds like a midlife crisis. Are you on Wall Street? Have you been hanging with Patrick Bateman again? You know that guy is coked out of his mind 90% of the time."

Laughter, and then, a cough, "You sound like you're doing well."

173

"I am," I said, and I meant it.

"I need to kick this smoking habit," he coughed again, "but other than that, I'm also doing *real* well. Business is… becoming." A pause. "Business is becoming a problem."

"Benihana's not doing well?"

"Oh, I moved on from that gig a bit ago. That's why I'm calling. One of the servers there told me someone was looking for me. I put the pieces together and figured it was you. I tried this number, the one Jiro had, and sure enough. You."

"Yeah it's still me. How is he?"

He changed the subject, "Business is becoming unwieldy, that's what I meant. Good problem to have sure, like smoking, until it threatens with cancer."

"You have cancer?"

"No, kid, keep up. I'm calling because you were looking for me." "It's true." I hit save on the Word doc, minimized it. Attention averted, current status: distracted. "But that was… however long ago it was. I call it my bender days."

"So you weren't doing so hot, huh?" He must have sensed the irritation in my voice, and sure—he existed to distract me, to be in my way. Even back when Jiro and I hung out, Garrett was the third wheel, the person that would get between a good conversation, always the one to steal the spotlight by buying the next round and making a big deal out of it. Same went for how he wouldn't tell me anything about Jiro, the entire call existing solely for him to field how I was doing. I bet he wondered if I had gone mad.

"I'm sorry to hear that."

It was my turn to change the subject. "A lifetime ago. What about Benihana? What pays the hooker bills these days?"

He didn't take to the joke this time, instead launching in a self-glorifying explanation about how he sold his stock in Benihana and invested in a new restaurant empire both overseas and domestically. He talked up the West Coast, specifically Los Angeles, how there's "money painting the streets." His words not mine. I half listened as I tended to Darcy.

It was time for that afternoon walk and right about now, I looked forward to the open expanse, the only eyes looking back at you were the hills in the distance, and not in that shitty slasher horror way.

He continued—the empire was doing so well, featured spots on Anthony Bourdain's Parts Unknown, taking the cuisine to the next level.

I kicked a plume of dirt, Darcy snapping at it. I grinned. Into the phone I had to ask, "What kind of cuisine?"

"Ever been outside of the country?"

Again, he gave me nothing.

"No, I can't say that I have."

A loud, sharp noise, Garrett's voice raised, a mock-heckle. The phone being palmed, no way I wanted to subject my ears to that shit.

"Kid, you owe it to yourself."

Kid. I owe a lot to others, but even more to myself. I owe myself mending from disrepair. No travel until I have transcended this trauma.

"Yeah," sure Garrett.

Instead, mind wandered and returned to the simple, persistent beauty of my surroundings. Historically, my attention was immediate, never more than a few steps ahead of me; traversing a city, I paid attention to who was in front, and behind, never who, what, and the wonder, a block ahead. It was as much the fire passing rather than the possible fire ahead.

What has changed? What was new?

Everything.

"Nothing," I said.

Everything, I felt safe in my own skin. These steps weren't being counted, there was no need. I enjoyed them for what they were, a walk, an excursion, a drifting into the delicate unknown. The trail was familiar by now, but in every walk Darcy and I had, there was a change, a difference. I might not have noticed these small, maybe insignificant switch-ups, but I was keen enough to be able to bear witness and appreciate them. I may never see a lizard skitter towards me, skin like leather, walking past me, regarding me with a past entirely their own. I appreciated what little I did have and held close the belief that I will have taken care of what I had when it finally leaves me.

"We should grab a drink sometime."

We arrived at the fork in the trail. Darcy stopped, waited for my choice. By now we were both heated, her making those noises she made, tongue out, panting. Me I had a visible sheet of sweat on the surface of my skin. My shirt peppered with damp spots, I looked at my phone. It too had the visible sheen of an overstated conversation. Enough was enough, I got the sense that Garrett called to brag. Just as anyone with an ego and a confidence problem does to balance each other out. He called me while walking from one thing to the next, not even the decency to call at his office, or when he had truly the time to listen.

Say anything but instead, I gave him as much as he gave me.

"I would but I'm off the sauce—"

He interrupted, "Good for you."

"…and I'm not currently in the city."

"Oh," he said it flatly, "you're not in the city." It might of, should have been, a question, instead it was more a statement.

"Santa Fe."

He asked what happened, "Bad breakup? A person leaves the city and its either for work or for personal reasons."

Wasn't that essentially the reason anyone did anything? People did things for work and for personal reasons. If it wasn't for either, people probably wouldn't do anything.

Sure, why not: I went with the flow, feel pity on me.

One moment, give it one real moment, and then I sighed.

Things on his end got quiet now, "What happened?"

One more pause and then—

"Legend of Zelda: Breath of the Wild."

176

I thought it was funny, but Garrett did not. We took a left at the fork, headed cliff-side. It went over his head, and he proceeded to babble, reaching for anything—it'll be okay, life is like that, you go through these cycles, and sometimes you feel so alive you forget that it'll one day feel like death, but you'll find someone else, what was it, Zelda? There'll be others to replace Zelda. Ups and downs, it's always ups and downs. "You will wake up one day... wait. I can't believe it. What was your name again? I'm so sorry, but I think I spaced it out. Wait, no. I never forget a name. You never told me." "Oh, I never told you?"

"No, you didn't."

Had I told anyone?

"It's Michael."

"Okay. I got to go. It was nice to rap. We should catch up, if you're ever back in the city..." He wanted off the phone ASAP, speaking quickly, leaving no room for me to react or interject, "And take care of yourself."

Take care of yourself.

"Bye, kid."

He didn't mean it, more of a figure of speech, but sure, why not?

How could I have forgotten to tell people my name?

Had I told you, all this time?

A perusal of the entire book, and you'll see that I found reason in keeping myself muted, silent, as though in not having a name saved me from having to finish this book. I didn't want to face the challenge, what had been identified as essential for this story to *have* a conclusion. In my name was the final and most devastating admission of having moved on, come to grips with our failures, and by that, I meant mine. It was not that I no longer cared about Jiro, because that couldn't be any further from the truth. It was more about the truth in plain, and the reality where we are never again friends, and being okay with that. That was how this worked. In revealing my name, I no longer had anything to hide behind.

The truth in plain: I know how to finish this book.

I wanted to live in it a little while longer.

FACES IN THE CROWD

W hat he was trying to tell me is, well, everything. He was trying to tell me that I wouldn't find him in these streets. That was for a previous fall, a season of transition and taking care of torment. Just like I had to eventually leave Santa Fe, I returned to the city, to the streets as another body traversing its textures. I had no expectations and demanded nothing more than maybe a path to walk. I started in deep Brooklyn, where some people wouldn't want to walk. But I did, and I listened and reacted, looking not through but at the various faces as I passed.

Some desired to provoke me. Some aimed for the opposite, grinning but seldom a wave. Most looked the other way, averting their gaze or worse, looked right through me. If there was anyone that understood why, it's the person writing this sentence.

The walk took me through the bowels of downtown Brooklyn, which always seemed humid, especially for the tail end of October. The density of the people walking Fulton Street was dizzying, but I remained steadfast, looking at everything around me. The smell was overwhelming, this one street must have had a block party because the people gathered like barricades preventing me from passing. The odor was strongly of grilling, and such was the sort of thing I would have almost run past, not because I wasn't curious but because I wouldn't even allow myself the acknowledgment of an activity. I was too anxious about the crowd, the act of being. All the anxiety about loneliness and, true to the conditions, I boxed myself into a zone of displacement. When lonely, you combat it by allowing yourself to be continually alone.

Take me to the bridge. The very same. But there weren't any memories now. Nothing of those moments, because they were already written and recorded here. This was a new day. I was back in the city, by choice. I walked of my own free will, with no clear destination other than the present action. Manhattan Bridge was as grungy as ever, spasming every couple minutes, the Q train passing through. I kept to a more relaxed pace, enough that people overtook me. Funny, I used to be the one that navigated through those with slower steps.

It was a happy thing, a moment to proclaim things were okay. I have no idea what awaits me in the future, much less what might become of this book, of myself, without a job, or really anywhere to stay passed the end of the month. But I had a roof over my head for the time being, and I had an idea of what tomorrow might be. That's all we can really hope for, right?

An idea, and the promise of more.

I walked in celebration. I walked because I had finished writing the book. The story was over, and still, the end of one story was the beginning of another, and the purpose of this walk was to seek out just that. Maybe I wouldn't find anything. That's okay.

Everything was once again new, as new and daunting as it was when I first started walking the city. The Bowery hadn't changed one bit. Some blocks had trash piled up so much that you couldn't avoid the puddles, the stench, the single file walk of the crowd around these nuisances. A powerful whiff of car exhaust as I finally made it to 4th Street.

It wouldn't be much longer now. Testament to not comprehending where you were heading until you get there, I found myself near

Union Square, making the same trek I had that evening I met Jiro. Where there had been a grand opening and a lot of activity, stood instead, a darkly painted storefront, dimly lit, and the activity you could say, kept to a lull. I didn't second guest it; this was where the restaurant had been. Like most things, it was temporary. The memory, fleeting, and all a person really had was the lasting impression. If there was one.

I stopped, looked up at the faux-Hollywood marquee, another bar, just what this city needed. On that street corner, literally ten steps away from where I now stood, I overheard Jiro talk about the now defunct restaurant. That was worth a chuckle. I guess he was right.

I walked inside, squinting as I waited for to get used to the dim lighting, I randomly chose a seat at the bar, distantly aware that I was in dangerous territory. This was how a person relapsed. But I wasn't worried. Didn't even skip a beat as I asked for a menu and told the bartender, "How about a coke?"

"Sure," the bartender winked, "preference of whiskey?"

I ignored the question.

She placed a hand on her waist, "Or let me guess, you're a bourbon type."

"I'm the coke-*only* type."

Someone overheard me, said "I could use some coke." Don't even bother. I wasn't in the mood. The bartender poured the coke, retaining eye contact with me, "So you're a foodie then?"

I looked at the menu, the usual bar food, my eye catching the description for the chili.

"Whenever I hear or read the word 'pouch,'" I looked up from the menu, "I cringe."

"And why is that?" She set the coke in front of me.

"Pouch. What is a pouch? Something that holds, but also what part of the body holds and retains? Stomach. Gut. Pouch. As in, that person has a pouch. Now replace pouch with gut. See what I mean?"

She laughed, "I take it you don't want the chili."

I paid for the coke in cash, 40% tip because hey, she was putting in an effort, good on her. It's difficult enough doing a job, much less doing it well, day in and day out. Who knows how far into her shift I caught her. "A brain holds and retains too. And part of me thinks you got a very interesting one." She retrieved the cash, again without breaking eye contact, "Definitely."

I nodded, waved goodbye, "Thanks." There was more to be said, but I left before it could be bookmarked and continued my walk. I looked over my shoulder, caught her looking at me, caught a good view of the entire bar. Give it time and this place too would turn into something else, maybe a Starbucks. Another Duane Reade.

I walked up Broadway until I reached 28th and then cut to 6th Avenue. From there it was a straight shot. Right to the park. Yup, that park. Central to everything, well not everything, but to the end of this experience. It has been so long since I walked Central Park at night.

At 57th street, I picked up the pace. Entering in from the south, I caught all the nostalgia, but none of the jealousy, none of the worry. I heard Jiro's voice, the long distant echoes of our discussions being fully and finally set free.

There was nothing left to be said. An interpretation first, adaptation later. I have adapted, but before I could—an interpretation. The reason art is so evocative is not because of what is set into ink, into frame, into the actual form. Rather, it's in how one consumes it, what they feel as they do, and how they embody the very thing that had embodied the artist.

You learn to interpret and then actualize the struggle of the dream.

At my feet, this was where he remained for a decade, not his body but surely his mind. It never left the confines of that metal box. Haunted by those memories, a person does so much to make do, but can seldom excel, move past it without first interpreting why, and how.

Jiro taught me more than he could have ever mustered in a single breath. He taught me that to live is to fail, and the only way to be reminded you're alive was to recognize that you could prove the world wrong, a single person against the billions, could actualize a dream.

You can show that every impossibility can be rendered possible. Think about where he might be at this very moment. And then say the words, first and final: Goodbye and hello. None too little, but enough. Enough to move on. To walk through the night, as rain clouds formed above me. But I would be okay. The subway was only a couple blocks away.

PARALLEL UNIVERSE

I have a job interview today. Part time work, but that's okay, I probably better to ease into things. A full-time job brings with it so much responsibility, and I have been alone in the desert for six months, barely saying a word to anyone but a canine companion. I tell myself it'll go well. I've done all that I can do. I scroll through the finished document before hitting print. I have three hours before I should leave for uptown, where the agency is, so I give the book one last skim, before finally and fully leaving it behind. At this length, it's going to take a lot of interest and effort for someone else to read it. I don't expect anyone should. I'm not asking, really. I wrote it out of a desire and a need, and whatever it is now, perhaps that is all it's going to be.

As I skim through, I tell myself that it's good.

I've done all that I can do.

I hit print, cringing at the thought of just how much ink this thing is going to take to print.

There is only one person that should know about the book, and I'm finally ready.

But not a phone call, the moment for that has passed. Instead a text, and in it, I don't apologize, not anymore, knowing well that if

185

he wanted to accept my apology, he would have accepted one of the dozens. Instead, I call it like it is, telling him of all that's happened since. Not the time in Santa Fe, or my low point, drinking and playing investigator. Save that for the book, if he needed to know. I tell him plainly that—I finished a book. It's about more or less all that happened between us. Moreover, it's about art, the struggle, depression, mostly my own, but I hoped that he wouldn't be mad that I sprinkled in a bit of his own suffering.

Talk of writer's block, it didn't wash clean, always muddied no matter how often I set out to write something, I couldn't keep to a scene. I couldn't be honest, not with myself, and not with the would-be reader. You are the reader, and I had written it for you from the beginning.

Between edits, life had its own ups and downs, as it always does, and it took me longer to get over the fact that you did not want me around, did not want me to know the conclusion of your own story, and so in the book, I gave you mine.

The inspiration never does make itself known, does it? It arrives unnoticed and you feed it neglect until you can learn to accept the challenges it has designed for you. When you conquer it, is there euphoria? I can finally tell you that there is. I actually finished something. It's being printed right now, before my very eyes. When the inspiration leaves you, everything and nothing is the same. I'll admit, I felt empty. The emptiness wasn't dissimilar from how I felt when I ran from you, ran from my own problems.

It really does feel like losing someone.

This book, it's no longer mine. I was just lucky enough to be the writer—wow I still can't get used to saying that—to have been able to put it into shape, every word second guessed until all the doubt became definitive.

By then, I was like you are when you make sushi, the whole world disappearing around you, and it's all there is, the sushi and in my case the sentence. You follow it like a drug, because the mending of the aftermath almost dares you into diving in, hiding from the emptiness.

Anyway, I wrote a book. It's partly about you. If you wanted to read it, please know that I would be honored to mail it to you. On my dime, of course.

Stupid, stupid, stupid—probably not the greatest of jokes but what's sent is sent.

I've done all that I can do.

With hours to kill, and anxious energy to quell, plus the weather is nice, I decided to go for a walk. It's getting cold out. I bet the city will experience its first snow in a few weeks, so every chance I have to get in some movement is a chance I shouldn't miss.

I've done enough missing for one year.

On impulse, I take the manuscript with me, because duh I am going to look it over again. Seeing it printed like this excites me, like it's suddenly more alive, a real thing.

The walk is pleasant enough, though I start to feel a little nostalgic. Not quite sad, though, but just... pining for something out of reach. No matter the distance time and growth provides there is always a certain nuance to some people, based entirely on experience, history, and, hell, just how you imagined them to be.

I duck into a park, needing a moment, distantly aware that I will begin looking through the printed manuscript, checking the time on my phone, only to notice I have a notification. I didn't even notice. Who is it from?

Jiro.

I exhale and then read the message. A single line that reads, "When will I read your work?" Also supplied is an address marked Tokyo, Japan. No analysis, not even a text message reply. I pocket my phone, feel the weight of the manuscript in my bag, and I proceed west, to the nearest UPS Store. I don't need to analyze how he will receive this book, just as I don't occupy my thoughts with debate on the level of sincerity of his question.

I walk to the store, double timing it because I don't want to be late for the interview, I see him everywhere. I see him in the elderly man on a park bench, hands folded, watching me as I pass. I see him in every single person standing impatiently on the street corner across from me, the memory of our own walks and how Jiro would unabashedly walk into the street though traffic still hadn't cleared enough for people to cross. I see him in the sushi restaurant I frequent, not because they do it well but rather because of the oddity with which the human senses worked—the smell of soy and sea urchin, so potent when done well you can taste it. And this isn't just nostalgia either. I stand in line to send out my story, and I don't forget to put my name in the return address.

Someone nearly collides into me as I walk past 32nd Street, a young woman shouting at the top of her lungs, "I got the part! I got the part!"

She apologizes, and of course I congratulate her.

"Thanks! Ahhhhh!" she shouts, we hug, and see, this is precisely how it has always been.

I am still meeting Jiro in every impassioned voice and vigilant spectacle of a person taking a risk for the sake of achieving their dreams. They brush aside the dreams of being and actively become, and I am still meeting Jiro in the hopeful face that will look back at me as they ask me who I am, what I have to offer, and ultimately, why I deserve this job. I am still meeting Jiro at the end of the day, on tired feet, yawning and wanting nothing more than to just watch Netflix instead of sitting down, once again, always, forever, at the desk, at the screen, staring at the start of the next paragraph. Within the desire that has become part of me, we continually meet.

I meet Jiro and what does he tell me? He tells me it's never too late. He tells me to keep writing. He tells me now to look, really look, at what I have just accomplished. In my bag, not weighing me down, but rather holding me up. He is right here, staring back at me.

BOOKS BY MICHAEL J SEIDLINGER

FICTION

My Pet Serial Killer

Falter Kingdom

The Strangest

Messes of Men

The Face of Any Other

Mother of a Machine Gun

The Fun We've Had

The Laughter of Strangers

The Sky Conducting

NONFICTION

Mark Z. Danielewski's House of Leaves: Bookmarked

POETRY

Standard Loneliness Package

MICHAEL J. SEIDLINGER is a Filipino American author of *My Pet Serial Killer, Dreams of Being, The Fun We've Had,* and nine other books. He has written for, among others, Buzzfeed, Thrillist, and Publishers Weekly, and has led workshops at Catapult, Kettle Pond Writer's Conference, and Sarah Lawrence. He is a co-founder and member of the arts collective, The Accomplices, and founder of the indie press, Civil Coping Mechanisms (CCM). He lives in Brooklyn, New York, where he never sleeps and is forever searching for the next best cup of coffee. You can find him online on Facebook, Twitter (@mjseidlinger), and Instagram (@michaelseidlinger).

9 780999 472354